CW00726619

WILD

FURY

PAUL ORTON

Copyright © 2021 Paul Orton

The right of Paul Orton to be identified as the Author of
the Work has been asserted by him in accordance with
the Copyright, Designs and Patents Act 1988.
All rights reserved.

Apart from any use permitted under UK copyright law, this
publication may only be reproduced, stored or
transmitted, in any form, or by any means with prior
permission in writing from the copyright holder or in the
case of reprographic production in accordance with the
terms of licences issued by the Copyright Licensing
Agency and may not be otherwise circulated in any form
of binding or cover other than that in which it is published
and without a similar condition being imposed on the
subsequent purchaser.

All characters in this publication are fictitious and any
resemblance to real persons, living or dead,
is purely co-incidental.

Font used for front cover, titles and chapter headings:
'Hacked' © David Libeau, used under Creative Commons
Licence.

"A little knowledge is a dangerous thing.
So is a lot."

Albert Einstein

PROLOGUE

Ryan shivered in the dark.

He huddled next to a tree, paralysed with fear. The other boy was coming for him. It was only a matter of time.

Way out here, in the wilderness, he didn't stand a chance. This wasn't some schoolboy grudge. This was the Fury. Two boys had been taken down, and Ryan was next.

He waited.

A twig snapped. He could hear someone creeping along a short distance away. And then he could see him out of the corner of his eye.

The boy's movements were wild and erratic. His twisted face glistened in the moonlight, burned and scarred.

'I'm going to kill you...'

The voice sounded evil. Demonic. This wasn't an idle threat. It was going to happen.

Ryan bolted, but he didn't get far. His socks slipped in the mud, making him easy prey. He was grabbed by the ankle and dangled upside down. He shielded his face with his arms as the lad started kicking him in the head.

Ryan cried out, screaming for the boy to stop.

Eventually, he did stop.

But by now, Ryan was sprawling in the dirt, helpless; beaten and bruised. He looked up to see the wild boy standing over him, holding a large branch, lifting it high like a club.

This is it, Ryan, he thought to himself. *This is where it ends.*

There was nothing he could do.

He closed his eyes and waited for the pain.

1. FAIL

'Wake up. WAKE THE HELL UP!'

They were shaking him by his shoulders.

Violently.

It took his brain a while to respond.

Ryan reached up to rub sleep from his eyes. Three vague outlines focused to become the angry faces of Kev, Lee and Jael; his roommates at Devonmoor academy.

'You're the worst, you know that?' Jael was clutching the back of his head with his hands.

'What? Am I late for drill?' Ryan propped himself up in bed, leaning on his arm. The others stood over him in their vests and boxers. 'Why aren't you guys dressed?'

Jael let out a muffled cry of frustration.

'Get up, Jacobs.' Kev's voice was hard. You didn't mess with Kev. At fourteen, a year older than Ryan, he was the leader. And if he called you by your surname, you knew you were in trouble.

Ryan figured he had better do as he was told. He slipped out from under the duvet and stood up. Kev grabbed his arm tight–way too tight–and dragged him over to the wardrobe. The doors were open, showing

7

nothing but bare wood and a lonely blue-and-yellow striped rugby shirt.

'Well?' demanded Kev. 'Where are our clothes? What the hell are we meant to wear?'

Ryan groaned. He was supposed to be on laundry duty. 'I forgot. I'm sorry.'

'YOU FORGOT?' Kev was right in his face. 'I reminded you at dinner yesterday! And the night before that!'

Ryan looked away, ashamed. 'Whatever.'

He knew that was like showing a red rag to a bull. The older boy would either give him a serious lecture on responsibility or hold him against the wall and beat him senseless.

Before either of those things happened, Lee glanced at the clock and broke them apart. 'Come on guys, we only have three minutes.'

Jael grabbed the laundry bin from the corner and emptied its contents over the floor. 'We'll have to re-use this stuff.'

'Just for the record,' said Kev, letting go of Ryan's arm, 'this is not over.'

Ryan reached down and grabbed himself some uniform from the pile. Every item reeked of sweat.

He looked over to see the grimace on Lee's face as the thin, blond-haired boy sniffed under the arm of his dark-grey military jacket.

'This is grim, Ryan,' said his best friend. 'Really grim.'

Ryan pulled on a pair of crumpled grey trousers, the other lads glancing at him as he got ready. They were sharp looks, full of anger and disappointment.

'Come on! Hurry!' Jael ushered them through the door and the four lads bolted to the drill hall. If they were even a few seconds late, the whole dorm would have to report an hour earlier the next day.

Devonmoor Academy was not a normal school, and life was tough here. You could get into trouble for almost anything, and often your roommates would be punished for something you did. Even food in the canteen was a privilege to be earned; some days you went hungry. Ryan had found that out the hard way. If you followed the rules, though, life here was also exciting. Every student was gifted or special and you got taught things you wouldn't learn in any other school, from flying helicopters to quantum maths.

The four lads reached the drill hall and marched in with a few seconds to spare. Ryan breathed a sigh of relief: if they'd been late, then his roommates would never have forgiven him.

The vast room doubled as a gym, and their footsteps echoed off the polished floor as the cadets took their place in line. There were several rows of students, all standing to attention, perfectly spaced from each other. They wore the same dark-grey military uniform with a thin maroon stripe down the side.

A clock at the front of the hall ticked round to seven-thirty and a loud buzzer sounded. The doors swung open, and Sergeant Wright strode in. He was clean shaven and his uniform was perfect.

'Morning, cadets,' he said.

'Good mor-ning sir,' everyone chanted in perfect unison. Ryan thought this routine was childish when he'd arrived—it reminded him of what they had to do in his primary school assembly.

Sergeant Wright walked up and down the rows, occasionally pausing to examine a cadet. He stopped in front of Kelvin Sparks, a rather overweight fourteen-year-old.

'Cadet Sparks, when did you last polish these boots?' he asked.

'Yesterday, sir. Honest.' Sparks sounded nervous, but he needn't have panicked; Wright was in a good mood.

'Well, lad,' he said. 'I suggest you get someone in your dorm to show you how to do it properly.'

'Yes, sir.'

The sergeant moved on. His heart didn't seem to be in the inspection, much to Ryan's relief, and he failed to notice the slipshod appearance of the lads from dormitory fourteen.

'We have a special announcement this morning, cadets,' he explained. 'Colonel Keller is here to give it to you.'

The colonel had entered the room and sat down while the younger officer was carrying out his inspection. Now he stood up.

Colonel Keller was the cruellest teacher at the academy, and he looked the part. He was a bear of a man. His face and neck showed several old scars, war wounds from ancient times.

While everyone feared the colonel, Ryan had

more reason than most. The man had hated Ryan from the moment they had met. He'd made Ryan's life hell and tried to get Ryan expelled from the academy. He rarely passed up an opportunity to pick on Ryan or make his life difficult.

'This week,' boomed the colonel, 'you will learn about teamwork. The ability to work well with others is central to the success of the Project. Students at this academy need the ability to share ideas and work collaboratively. Normal lessons are suspended all week. As of now, you are on a special timetable. After three days of school-based work, we will test your teamwork on a two-day hike. We have selected teams for you, and we will display these on the noticeboard at lunchtime.' The colonel narrowed his eyes and lowered his voice a little, almost hissing as he continued. 'Be assured that this is not some kind of fun diversion. If your team come last, or if they fail to complete the hike, then you will receive remedial teamwork classes until the *necessary* lessons have been learned, however long that takes.' He turned and strode from the room, leaving the threat hanging in the air.

'Well,' said Sergeant Wright, 'you heard the colonel. Check the timetable outside for your first lesson. And prepare yourselves for what's ahead. Dismissed.'

Ryan found himself next to Jael as they filed out.

'I hope I'm not on your team,' muttered Jael. 'I want to work with people who pull their weight.'

'Whatever.'

Whoever he ended up with, Ryan knew one thing: he needed to keep his head down and ensure that he didn't end up doing any remedial teamwork classes with the colonel. He dreaded to think about what they would involve, but he knew it wouldn't be good.

Especially for him.

2. MADNESS

According to the special timetable, Ryan's first lesson was science. He wasn't sure how that linked with the whole teamwork theme, but he dutifully made his way up to the classroom.

The science labs at Devonmoor weren't like those in a normal school. There were still rows of stools and benches, and racks of test tubes and equipment, but there were also computer screens embedded into every desk and numerous pieces of high-tech equipment within easy reach. Sun streamed through the windows along one side.

At the back of the room there was a door through to an animal testing area, where a variety of creatures—mainly rats, mice and monkeys—were kept in cages. Ryan felt sorry for the animals, but it wasn't like anyone cared about his opinion. They were needed for scientific experiments. Various scratching noises and monkey cries filtered through to the main classroom, but the students were used to them by now. And for once, Ryan was glad of the strong animal smell as it hid the odour of stale sweat from his uniform.

Because of the new timetable, the class had a

strange mix of students. James Sarrell was one of them—an older cadet who had bullied him since he arrived at Devonmoor. Ryan hoped that if he kept his head down, then Sarrell wouldn't notice him. Lee was also in the class, but had found himself a seat near the centre of the room, probably still annoyed at Ryan.

Mr Cho stood at the front wearing his white lab coat. A data-projector cast a dark blue background onto the whiteboard. On it were the words: "Co-operation vs. Competition: The problem of Teamwork in Evolution."

Once the cadets had taken their seats, Mr Cho clapped his hands together twice and there was instant silence.

'Good morning, cadets.' He spoke quietly, but was wearing a small wireless microphone on his lab coat, which amplified his voice. He didn't expect or wait for a response. 'I have been asked to present to you a scientific view on teamwork, which is something of a problem. Science does not have a view on teamwork. I cannot tell you that science suggests teamwork is a good thing, because such value judgements lie outside the realms of scientific enquiry. However, it is acceptable for us to ask how teamwork affects animal populations. So, this morning we will look at the advantages and disadvantages of such teamwork in nature.'

He clicked a small device he was holding. The screen showed two lists. Under the heading 'Species A' was a brief description: 'Highly competitive and selfish. Members of this species work alone.' Meanwhile, 'Species B' was described as: 'Very co-operative. Members of this species work with others and act selflessly to protect the common good.'

'We have an interesting question before us as scientists,' continued Mr Cho. 'Which of these two species should survive for longer? You have all studied evolution, and you will be aware of how we talk about the "survival of the fittest" to suggest that the strongest and most selfish individuals within any given species are likely to be rewarded. Over time, the whole species becomes better suited to its environment. Such a system seems to be weighted towards competition.' There was a strange clanging noise at the back of the class, which momentarily distracted Mr Cho, but seeing no cause for it, he pressed on. 'But the odd thing is that the species which are the least selfish are those which thrive in nature. How can we explain that? Why does one kind of animal fight its own kind, but another work in harmony with its brothers and sisters? Given the process of natural selection, why would any animals lay down their lives for their packs or their colonies?'

The screen changed again. A large picture of an ant colony appeared. Mr Cho was opening his mouth to speak when there was a blood-curdling scream from the back of the room that sent a shiver down Ryan's spine.

He turned to see a blur of brown fur launch itself into the middle of the seated students. A monkey had broken free from its cage and was flinging itself from desk to desk, swinging its arms. A few of the cadets got nasty scratches as it leapt around, shrieking with rage. Lee cried out as the monkey's paw caught him across the face, leaving a bright red streak of blood.

Then, in a whirlwind of limbs, the wild beast flew straight at Mr Cho. The science teacher froze as the animal grabbed his neck and bit his face. Man and monkey fell to the floor in a surreal wrestling match. It was a contest between wild nature and meticulous order. From the quantity of blood, it appeared that nature was winning.

Most students had backed away from the crazed animal, clinging to the edges of the classroom for some kind of protection. Sarrell, however, did the opposite. He was at Mr Cho's side in seconds, pulling the monkey off. Sarrell's hands wrapped around the animal's throat and the monkey had no choice but to let go of Mr Cho and to aim its attack at the cadet, hissing and spitting.

Sarrell held it in front of him, at arm's length, staring it in the eye. He ignored the pain as the claws scratched at his arms. The animal's eyes went from wide to narrow, then back again. It made frantic noises, contorting its limbs in strange and unnatural ways, trying to break free. But Sarrell was cold, expressionless. He didn't move as he held the monkey by the neck.

Then, with a sickening crack, the monkey let out a low moan and went limp, its neck broken. Sarrell dropped it to the floor and nudged it with his foot. He reached down to help Mr Cho to his feet, blood dripping from his scratched arms.

'Are you ok, sir?' he asked, as the other students gathered round.

'Yes, yes,' said Mr Cho, trying to stand. The teacher was in a state of shock; the monkey had taken a chunk out of his cheek and he appeared to be on the brink of passing out.

'Listen up,' said Sarrell. 'Cadet Jeet, fetch help for Mr Cho. Everyone else can go for a break. Clear out of the room. If you're injured, then head straight to the medical room. Does everyone understand?'

The cadets nodded, gathered their stuff, and headed off. Two older cadets hung back with Sarrell to look after the teacher until help arrived.

Ryan made his way down the stairs, following the others to the common room. Everyone spoke in hushed tones.

'Did you see Cho's face?'

'He looked like he lost half of it!'

'What was with Sarrell as he stared the monkey down?'

'He's insane! He didn't seem to care that it was scratching his arms to pieces.'

'But how did it escape in the first place?'

As they made their way along the corridor, Ryan couldn't help feeling that this was going to be a really strange week.

But even he couldn't guess what lay ahead.

3. TEAMS

Outside the school canteen, a crowd of students had gathered by the noticeboard. Ryan pushed forward and scanned it for his name, hoping he had a decent team.

He was on Team 7 with Sarah Devonmoor, Jael Marquez and Hannah Green.

It could be worse. Sarah was the oldest in the group at sixteen. She was the granddaughter of Lady Devonmoor—the academy's kind and elderly headteacher—but Sarah always appeared cold and detached to Ryan. He got the impression she didn't like him much. Still, she would be keen to win, and she'd be an excellent leader.

As for the rest of the team, he barely knew Hannah. She was a year or two younger and always seemed to keep to herself. Jael was one of Ryan's closest friends, although they had something of a love-hate relationship, especially at the moment. Jael would hold a grudge about the laundry failure, and Ryan knew he'd have to work extra hard to ensure that they were on good terms.

Overall, though, it was good news. He made his way to lunch, hungry after a long morning.

The canteen was light and airy, full of polished steel tables and pot plants. Huge windows overlooked the school playing fields and modern artwork adorned the walls. The smell of cooked meat hung heavy in the air and students flocked towards it.

A prefect blocked their way. 'Go straight to your tables,' she ordered.

Normally, students collected their food and then chose where to sit, but today, things were going to work differently. Ryan noticed the tables had been labelled with the team numbers. He couldn't remember his, but Jael had already sat down at 'Team 7', so Ryan joined him.

Jael glanced up at Ryan, then sighed and looked away. 'Of all the students at the academy, I had to end up with you,' he muttered. 'Typical.'

'Look, I'm sorry, ok?' urged Ryan, keen to resolve things. 'I'll make it up to you, I promise. Don't let a few dirty clothes affect the team or the hike or anything. You know we can't afford to lose this. It's not worth it.'

'Ok.' Jael looked him in the eye. 'You're on. But if you mess this up for us, then I'm going to make your life a living hell.'

Ryan wanted to argue, but he stopped himself. 'Fine.'

On the table across from them, Ryan could see that Kev and Lee were on the same team as each other, along with a younger girl called Kirsty Riggs and an older lad, Mark Collins. Kirsty was a science genius, and Mark was a strategist. It was a strong team.

'Do you think we stand a chance at winning this thing?' he asked Jael as he looked around.

Hands tightened on Ryan's shoulders from behind, digging in so tight he cried out in pain. Long brown hair brushed by his ear, and he looked up to see the stern face of Sarah Devonmoor.

'Cadet Jacobs,' she said. 'I think we need to get one thing clear from the start, don't you? We *are* going to win. Losing is not an option. Coming second is not an option. On this team we will eat, sleep and breathe success. You will give me one hundred percent of your effort and energy, and you will not complain. If we come first, then, and only then, will you have earned my respect. Do you understand?'

'Yes, ma'am,' replied Ryan, holding back the tears.

'Good boy.' She let go of his shoulders and settled on the bench next to him. Hannah arrived and sat next to Jael.

'Hi Hannah,' smiled Sarah, all sweetness and light. 'It's so good to have you on the team. I hear you're a geography buff?' She gave a sideways glance at Ryan. Sarah was messing with his head, but he had no idea why. Hannah, however, was unaware of this and smiled back, shyly. She obviously thought that Sarah was going to be the nicest team leader in the world.

There was the sound of cutlery being banged on a table, and the room fell silent. Colonel Keller stood at the front, looking mean as always.

'Well, cadets,' he boomed, 'it all begins here. This

week we will test your teamwork to the very limit. We thought we'd start the process right now. You must be hungry? But not all of you are going to eat. Instead, one member of each team is going to miss out on lunch and will report to the drill hall. It's up to you as teams to work out who that is, but your team leader's decision is final. Leaders, you have three minutes to make your selection.'

The colonel sat down and everyone started talking at once.

'Well, I wonder who that's going to be.' Sarah looked at Ryan, raising her eyebrows.

He groaned. 'Any reason it's me?'

'Maybe because you're a cocky little git?'

Jael laughed out loud. 'She's got your number, Ryan.'

'And there's no room for discussion on this?'

'None,' said Sarah. 'Have fun.'

'Fine. But just so you know, *Sarah*, this sucks!' Ryan made his way towards the canteen door where the colonel was waiting. A few others followed. Kev was among them. Knowing him, he'd done the honourable thing of volunteering to miss out on lunch for the sake of his team. That didn't make Ryan feel any better.

Once the three minutes were up, Ryan and the other unlucky cadets followed the colonel down to the drill hall, where they lined up along the back wall.

'Attention!' ordered the colonel. He paced up and down in front of them as he spoke. 'I don't know if you volunteered to be here, or if your teammates sent you, but I am going to make each of you an offer. You can choose to go back to the canteen and eat a full meal. However, if you do that, then the rest of your team will end up here instead. You have one minute to decide. If you want lunch, all you have to do is step forward.'

This was typical of the colonel. He enjoyed his little mind games. But you had to give it to the cadets— no-one moved. The colonel continued goading them. 'Just to be clear, if you don't step forward, then you will remain here throughout the lunch period. If you move an inch, then your entire team will miss their lunch for the rest of the week. You have forty seconds left to decide.'

Ryan knew he was serious, but he also knew that he couldn't step forward, however tempting it was. Any remaining hope that he might get something to eat faded, and the hunger seemed to grow.

The colonel was enjoying himself. 'Are you sure you want to do this? You only have twenty seconds left.' He looked up and down the line, glancing at his watch. 'Ten, nine, eight, seven... last chance to escape!'

Still no-one moved.

'Four... three... two... one... The offer has expired. I'm impressed. Teamwork involves self sacrifice, and it seems you are all very team-spirited today. However, I think we'll repeat this exercise and see if any of you reconsider. I expect to see you all back here at lunchtime tomorrow. In the meantime, you have forty-nine minutes to enjoy. While you're standing here, your teammates are sitting down to a cooked meal. Afterwards, they'll head to the common room, relax for a bit, chat with each other. I wonder if they even care that you're here? Worth thinking about, isn't it?'

With that, the colonel turned and left, leaving a prefect watching the unfortunate cadets.

4. LOSING

'Jacobs! Jacobs! Over here!'

It was the middle of the afternoon and Ryan was on the school field, playing football. The sky was grey, and it had begun to rain.

Ryan could see his teammate, Drew, running up the side of the pitch, calling for the ball. But he didn't need to pass: the goal was mostly unprotected. Only the keeper stood in his way. As he reached the box, he struck the ball hard, aiming for the bottom right corner.

It was a decent shot, but the other team had Lee in goal, who had fast reflexes and blocked it with his foot. The ball hit Ryan hard in the face and he fell to his knees in the mud.

Sergeant Wright blew a whistle and ran over to check on him. 'Are you alright, Jacobs?'

'Ye-yes, sir.' Ryan dragged himself back up, wiping his hands on his shirt.

Lee stepped forward and offered him his hand. 'Sorry Ryan. Didn't mean to do that.'

That was a relief. Ryan hadn't been sure if it was deliberate. 'It's fine. I'm ok.'

He straightened up. He could see Drew

approaching out of the corner of his eye. The younger boy was furious.

'What the hell, Ryan? You should have passed! I had a clear shot! You *never* pass!'

Ryan ignored him and turned away, knowing that Drew was right but not being willing to admit it. He had wanted to score. Now, they only had a few minutes of the game left, and that was probably the last chance they were going to get.

Sure enough, the other side were making their way up the field and it was as if Ryan's team had given up. Their goal was under attack from no less than four players wearing red training vests, and there wasn't a defender in sight. It was no surprise when the ball ended up in the back of the net.

'WHERE'S OUR DEFENCE?' shouted Ryan, frustrated.

'Shut up and get back here, Jacobs!' responded one of his teammates from the other end of the pitch. 'Stop goal-hanging!'

Ryan decided there was no point. It was too late.

A few minutes later, Sergeant Wright blew hard on the whistle and the lads gathered round. 'Reds, well done. Go and shower. Blues, today's session was about teamwork and you boys need to learn to work together! It was a shambles! So bad, in fact, that you owe me five laps of the field. No cutting corners.'

The losing team groaned and set off.

'This is your fault, Jacobs,' said Adams as he ran alongside him in the rain. 'You should have passed.'

'He never passes,' added Jason. 'I had three clear

shots but he wouldn't send me the ball.'

'That's because I've seen you play,' said Ryan, but he knew it was a weak response.

He dropped back a little to calm down and found himself jogging beside Kev. 'Hey,' he said, hoping that his roommate was still talking to him.

'Well,' said Kev, shaking his head, 'that was shocking.'

'Yeah, we didn't do so good.'

'We? It was mostly your fault, Ryan!' Kev sounded frustrated.

'What! How come?'

'Gee, let me think. You shout at everyone else, but you don't put any work in. You're only interested in scoring, so you leave the midfield empty. And most of all, you never pass!'

Ryan opened his mouth to respond, but carried on in silence as he thought about what the older lad was saying.

Kev sighed, before adding: 'The truth is you're not a bad player, Ryan. But you're a terrible *team* player.'

That comment hurt. Ryan had huge respect for Kev, especially in sports. After all, the boy had captained the England under-12's rugby squad before coming to the academy. 'Is that why you never pick me to be on the school team?'

'Pretty much.' Kev's voice was softer now.

'Ok, ok.' Ryan wiped rain from his face with his sleeve. 'I'll work on it. I promise.' He looked sideways and forced a smile at Kev, trying to ease the tension. 'And at least I'll learn loads about teamwork from the colonel this week.'

Kev gave in and smiled back. 'I'm sure you'll be his favourite student!'

***

Jael and Lee had already showered and were pulling on their academy uniforms by the time Ryan got back to the changing room.

'Pleasant run?' asked Jael, a slight edge to his voice.

'Shut up.' Ryan wasn't in the mood. He pulled off his damp shirt and sat down on one of the wooden benches.

Jael wouldn't let it go. 'That was another amazing display of teamwork from you out there.'

'I said drop it!' Ryan stood up, getting right in Jael's face. 'I don't need this right now! I'm tired, I'm hungry and EVERYONE IS ON MY CASE!'

At that precise moment, Ryan felt a sharp pain on his back and turned to see Drew standing there with a wet towel. 'What the—'

THWACK!

Drew whipped the towel at Ryan again, catching him high on the torso and leaving a red mark.

'STOP THAT!' Ryan covered his chest with his arms, feeling vulnerable.

'Why should I listen to you, Jacobs? You didn't listen to me on the pitch.'

THWACK!

This time the towel caught Ryan on the leg, and

27

he cried out in pain, backing up against a wall. He looked to Jael for support, but his roommate held up his hands. 'Hey, if you enjoy working on your own so much, deal with it.'

Great.

Ryan turned to face his attacker.

Drew was a little younger than Ryan, but he was tough and wiry; a weasel of a boy. Ryan wasn't sure if he could take him. Besides, he had a couple of his friends standing beside him, and there was no way Ryan could fight them all.

THWACK!

'I think you owe us an apology, Jacobs, don't you?'

Drew knew how to inflict pain. Ryan was cowering in the corner of the changing rooms, one arm outstretched.

'Ok, ok,' his voice trembled as he spoke. 'I'm sorry. Alright?'

'Did you hear that, lads? He's sorry.' Drew had an evil smile as he turned away.

As Ryan lowered his guard, the lad turned around and aimed one more shot, this time at his privates. Ryan crumpled to the floor, holding back tears as the pain registered.

'Aw, man up Jacobs.'

The boys laughed. One of them prodded Ryan with his foot, wiping the mud off his boot. Meanwhile, Drew turned and grabbed Ryan's uniform off the bench.

'Well, what do we have here?' he said. He sniffed it and made a face. 'You really do stink, Jacobs.'

Ryan wanted the floor to open up and swallow him. No-one in the changing rooms came to his defence, not even Kev.

'This uniform needs a wash.' Drew took the pile of clothes over to the showers and threw them in. The lads who were in there started kicking them around for a laugh.

Drew turned his attention back to Ryan, still holding his towel. 'Now say thank you, Jacobs.'

Ryan couldn't see any way out of it. 'Thank you.'

His humiliation was complete. He'd been beaten up by a kid who was younger than him and then thanked him for the privilege. Meanwhile, everyone else stood and watched. They probably all thought he deserved it.

'Later,' spat Drew, heading out the changing room, his friends trailing behind him.

Once they'd gone, Ryan looked up at Jael. He let his anger surface. 'Happy now? I'm surprised you didn't join in! I'm still here on the floor if you want to kick me or anything?'

'Hey, don't blame me.' Jael shrugged. 'You brought that on yourself.'

Ryan, sulking and in pain, edged himself back onto the bench. He pulled off his muddy socks and shin pads, his face burning.

Kev dropped a load of dirty sports kits in front of him. 'Err, I know this isn't a good time,' he said, 'but you need to do all of our laundry today, these included.'

Ryan wasn't in the mood to argue. 'Fine. Anything

else?'

'Hey, it's nothing personal,' said Kev. 'It's just your turn. And we're sick of wearing dirty clothes.'

Ryan didn't respond. He sat back while Kev headed into the showers. He hadn't been in this much trouble at the academy since he first arrived. Now it seemed everyone hated him again.

He was going to have to crack this teamwork thing. Even if it killed him.

5. EMPTY

The laundry room at Devonmoor was tucked away in the basement. It wasn't a great place to be at the best of times. Ryan stepped over dirty clothes and ducked under damp uniforms that hung from long washing lines.

He hauled the dirty sports kit over to one of the large machines and stuffed it in, wrinkling his nose in disgust. Grabbing an enormous box of washing powder, he poured some into the drawer. He wasn't sure which setting he needed, but no-one seemed to change them much anyway, so he pressed 'START' and heard the machine whir into life.

A couple of other machines were empty too and Ryan figured he might as well fetch the rest of the washing from his dorm and get it done at the same time.

The academy was quiet—too quiet for this time of day. Usually, after the last lesson finished, there would be people milling about, heading between the dorms and the common room, or going to the library to study, but Ryan didn't see anyone.

His feet squelched as he made his way along the corridor. The thick grey socks were soaking wet, along with everything else. He'd considered staying in his football kit but it was filthy and you weren't allowed to wear sports clothes in the main building. Devonmoor was strict over trivial stuff like that, and the last thing he needed was to get into more trouble. So, he'd wrung out his clothes and tried to dry them under the hand-driers as best he could before pulling them on. Now he was damp and uncomfortable.

The dorm was empty when Ryan arrived. He was relieved that he wouldn't have to cope with any sarcastic remarks from Jael or the others. The over-full laundry bin felt heavy, but he picked it up and carried it down the corridor towards the basement. Ryan hated handling the other lads' dirty socks and boxers: it freaked him out. But it wasn't like he had a choice. He crammed everything in to the washing machines and set them going.

Now what?

He had an hour until they were finished and he didn't intend to spend it down here. It wasn't too difficult a decision. He headed along the basement corridor to the computer lab. He was surprised to discover that was empty as well. The last time he'd seen anyone was in the changing room. By the time he'd showered and sorted out his wet clothes, he'd been the last person to leave.

And everyone else had disappeared.

Where were they?

Should he even care?

The calm hum of the machines seemed to call out to him, and he made his way over to his favourite computer in the corner, under the metal gantry that ran along the back of the room. He'd only just logged on when he heard a familiar whistle and Mr Davids strolled in.

'Ah, Ryan, my boy!' said the teacher, re-adjusting his thick spectacles. 'Good to see you, good to see you!'

'Hi, sir.'

During the past few minutes, Ryan had become aware of his growing hunger. Mr Davids was the only teacher at the academy he could ask. 'Sir, I don't suppose you have any food I could have, do you? I kind of skipped lunch.'

Most teachers would have known that students missed out on meals for a reason, but Mr Davids wasn't your usual member of Devonmoor staff. He opened a drawer in his desk and rooted around, pulling out a chocolate bar. 'Here you go, my lad. I always find chocolate helps me to think, yes?'

'Definitely! Thank you, sir.' Ryan couldn't believe his luck as he headed over to the teacher's desk. He ripped off the wrapper and started eating. 'Do you know where everyone else is?'

'Everyone else? Hmm.' Mr Davids looked puzzled, as if he'd been set a complicated riddle. 'No, no, I have no idea. But never mind that! I think I may be on the verge of a breakthrough, Ryan. I am so close. Want to see, yes?'

'Sure.' Ryan headed round the desk. 'What is it?'

Mr Davids pointed to a screen full of complex computer code. 'Take a look.'

Ryan leaned forward, his face close to the monitor. To most people, the code would have been meaningless: endless strings of random letters and numbers, with the odd recognisable word. But Ryan's eyes scanned the screen at an impressive speed. He reached across and scrolled down.

'Impressive, yes?' chuckled the teacher.

'It—it looks like a virus. A powerful virus.' Ryan was transfixed.

'Yes, yes! Check this piece out!' Mr Davids pointed like an excited child showing off a new toy.

Ryan was already studying that piece of code. He worked through it in his mind, going over it several times, trying to figure out what it would do. 'Is that a fractal equation?' he asked, his forehead creased in concentration.

'Very good! Very good! Yes! I call it the Chaos Flower!' Mr Davids beamed. 'Isn't it beautiful?'

Ryan could just about grasp it. Mr Davids had created a program that could plant and grow itself in a system. The Chaos Flower was a good name. He shook his head and looked at his teacher, concerned. 'But sir, it's a virus; a dangerous virus.'

Mr Davids smiled. 'No, Ryan, it's an *antivirus*. It operates like a virus, spreading from machine to machine, but instead of infecting them, it does the opposite. The Chaos Flower will be the last line of defence in the data war. If anyone slips a virus into the Ministry of Defence system, or any other critical system come to that, then we let this baby out of its box!'

That made more sense. 'It's awesome.'

The teacher shook his head. 'Unfortunately, it's not finished. There's a crucial piece I can't crack.' He scrolled further down. 'Once the antivirus is in the system, it needs to locate any virus and then combat it. Finding the virus isn't too difficult, see?'

Ryan scanned the code. 'I think so.'

'But once you know what's been corrupted, you need to change it back. That's easy for most viruses. But what if it's a level five infection? What if it hides its own history? What if it corrupts its own corruption?'

Ryan's head was spinning. 'If it's a level five, then you have to format the hard-drive and start again,' said Ryan. 'It's a rule. You can't undo that kind of damage.'

Mr Davids didn't agree. 'It's all maths and patterns, Ryan. You know that! There must be a way! There must!'

'I guess so.' Ryan was unconvinced, but respected the teacher enough not to contradict him. 'Good luck with that, sir.'

The teacher had already turned his attention back to the monitor and was deep in thought. He'd forgotten anyone else was there.

Ryan smiled and headed back to his own desk, pulling up some code he was working on. But he struggled to focus.

Two minutes later, the door to the lab swung open and Jael stormed in, his face like thunder. 'RYAN! I knew you'd be skiving in here! You're meant to be in a meeting!'

'What? What meeting?' Today was getting weirder and weirder.

'Stop playing dumb.' Jael wasn't in the mood to explain. 'Sarah's fuming mad.'

'Ok, ok, I'm coming.' Ryan logged off and stood up. 'Sorry. I didn't know, alright?'

Jael didn't look any happier. 'I think you're gonna have to come up with something better than that.'

***

'Cadet Jacobs, how nice of you to join us.' Sarah's voice dripped with sarcasm. If looks could kill, then Ryan would have died right there.

'Sorry.' He pulled up a chair and sat down in the empty classroom. Jael did the same. Hannah and Sarah were holding sheets of paper. They looked like they'd been hard at work.

'Is there any reason you missed most of our team meeting?'

'I didn't know about it! I thought lessons ended at four, like usual.' Ryan was frustrated. This was the last thing he needed right now.

'And you didn't think to check the special timetable at all? Like everyone else?' Sarah was going to draw this out, to make him suffer. Jael watched with a satisfied look in his eyes; he was just as angry. Only Hannah looked uncomfortable.

'No, I didn't check the timetable and I should have done. It won't happen again, ma'am.' You were meant to refer to prefects as 'sir' or 'ma'am' and Ryan hoped that the sign of respect might calm Sarah down.

She leaned back in her seat, like a medieval queen deciding whether to behead a peasant. 'Are you committed to this team?' she asked.

'Absolutely.' Ryan said it as convincingly as he could. He shivered a little because of his damp uniform. 'It was a genuine mistake. I'll work my butt off to ensure that we win. I promise.'

'You'd better, Jacobs.' Sarah leaned over and handed him two sheets of paper. 'Read these.'

Ryan glanced down at the information.

At 3.00pm on Thursday, all students will be taken to a starting location to begin a thirty-mile hike. The hike must be completed as soon as possible, and by 10.00pm on Friday at the latest. Teams should note that the terrain will be difficult, and that they will need to cross a river.

Each team member will wear their usual academy uniform, and will be given a rucksack containing:
- *Roll mat*
- *Sleeping bag*
- *Survival bag*
- *Whistle*
- *Torch*
- *Waterproof trousers + jacket*
- *1 x thermal t-shirt*
- *1 x spare pair of socks*
- *1 x spare underwear*
- *Food + drink*

Each group will also receive:
- *2 x tents*
- *First aid kit*
- *Compass*
- *Stopwatch*
- *2 x emergency flares*
- *1 x penknife*

It seemed straightforward enough. Ryan had never been camping, let alone on a hike, but if they provided all the equipment, then he wasn't too worried. Thirty miles was some distance, but it must be possible. He carried on reading.

Each team will spend significant time preparing for the hike itself. They will design, make or build a single item (or multiple identical items) that will help them complete the hike faster. Such items may include, but are not limited to: clothing, vehicles or technology.

Each team can use materials available in the school science and technology labs, and any items must be designed and put together solely by them.

On Monday and Tuesday, teams will need to choose what they intend to take with them, and design it. A teacher will meet with each team on Tuesday afternoon to discuss their final requirements and approve the exact materials needed.

On Wednesday, teams will make or build their item(s) ready for the hike.

Ryan looked up.

'Well?' demanded Sarah.

'Errrr, yeah, ok. I think I get it,' Ryan said. 'We get

to design something that will help us finish the hike quicker. So what ideas do we have?'

'*We* have several good ideas,' said Sarah. '*You*, on the other hand, have yet to make any significant contribution to the team.'

'Hey, hold up. I missed out on lunch for all of you!' objected Ryan.

'Only because I made you.' Sarah didn't know that the students in the drill hall had been given any options. 'It wasn't like you volunteered.'

Ryan opened his mouth to correct her, but then closed it again. He wanted to keep it secret; it felt more noble.

'Ok,' he sighed, defeated. 'I'm a terrible team player; I get it. I screwed up like I always do. And you're going to keep going on about it. So why not tell me what happens next? What do I have to do?'

'That's simple,' replied Sarah. 'Come up with some ideas for what we can take with us on the hike. Good ideas that will help us win. And then we can discuss them at our meeting tomorrow. I think three quality ideas should be enough.'

Ryan was taken aback. 'But aren't we meant to do that together?'

'Yes.' Sarah stared him down. 'And if you'd been here at four o'clock, that's what we'd have done. As it is, we've already come up with stuff. Now it's your turn. And they better be good ideas, Jacobs. *Really* good ideas.'

Ryan crossed his arms. 'Fine.'

'I'd hate it if we weren't seeing eye to eye when I'm

responsible for your dorm inspection next term.' Sarah smiled coldly.

Ryan could imagine what that would be like: *Jacobs, your bed isn't made correctly, do it again. This floor is filthy; it needs scrubbing! When was this toilet last cleaned?*

She had him cornered, and she knew it. 'And Jacobs, is there a reason your uniform is wet?'

'I sort of dropped it in the shower,' lied Ryan.

'You dropped it in the shower?' Sarah raised her eyebrows, as if he was a complete idiot.

'Yeah. Sorry.' Ryan wasn't sure why he needed to apologise.

Sarah shook her head before leaving the room, followed by Jael and Hannah. Ryan was left alone, water dripping from his trouser legs and jacket sleeves onto the tiled floor.

Even by Devonmoor's standards, this was turning out to be a seriously bad day.

6. BET

By the time the cadets sat down for dinner, Ryan was desperately hungry and no closer to coming up with any ideas.

He'd at least got his dorm's uniforms out of the washing machines and into the dryers, so he was on track for getting clean clothes to his roommates by the end of the evening. Meanwhile, his own battered uniform had mostly dried out, but it had a strange odour: a mixture of sweat and soap.

He took his place next to Sarah, Jael and Hannah.

'How are the ideas coming, Jacobs?' asked Sarah. 'Anything to share with us yet?'

'Not yet,' he muttered.

'The clock's ticking.' She gave him a warning look and then ignored him for the rest of the meal.

While he ate, Ryan kept glancing over to the table on his right where Lee and Kev sat with Kirsty and Mark, laughing and joking. Kirsty was pouring drinks for them and Mark was telling a funny story. They all seemed full of life and energy; they were the loudest table there.

He was glad to slip away as soon as the meal finished. He headed to the common room. As he walked along the corridor, Kev caught up with him.

'Hey, Ryan, how's your team doing?'

'Yeah, great.'

'So, you and Jael haven't killed each other yet?'

'Not yet. It probably will happen though, at some point.' Ryan smiled at him. 'We'll still win.' He wasn't sure why he was being so cocky, but his mouth seemed to decide for him.

'That's fighting talk!' laughed Kev. 'Good luck with that.'

'We won't need luck,' shot back Ryan. 'I'm on the team.'

'Yeah,' said Kev, giving him a sideways glance, 'but you know as well as I do, teamwork is not your strong suit.'

The lads had arrived at the common room and they settled into the comfortable sofas in the corner, tucked away behind the roof beams. Warm spotlights illuminated the sloping ceiling and a music channel played on the TV.

As they sat down, a crazy idea popped into Ryan's head and he blurted it out: 'How about we make a bet? If I prove you wrong… if I prove I can work as part of a team, then you guys lay off me and I get off doing laundry for the rest of the term?'

'What? You mean if you beat our team on the hike?' Kev looked amused.

'Yeah. I reckon my team can do it.' Ryan wasn't sure where his bravado was coming from.

'Ryan, I'll tell you what. If your team pull together and you get back before us then I will happily pick up the *whole* dorm's laundry duty for the rest of term. But if you lose, then you have to do it. All of it. No whining and no complaints. Ok?'

Ryan wanted to say no; a small voice at the back of his brain knew that he should never agree to this bet. It was insane. His team was already falling to pieces. And he hated doing the laundry with a passion.

He hesitated, stalling for time. 'What about Jael and Lee?'

'They won't mind,' pointed out Kev. 'Either you end up doing it all or I do. They get off either way.'

'That's hardly fair.'

'No, but it doesn't bother me, because I have no intention of losing. And if you're so sure you'll win, then it shouldn't bother you either.'

Ryan was cornered. 'Ok. You're on.' He said it before he could stop himself.

Kev shouted some guys over. 'Hey, Ranjit! Sparks! Lee! Get over here, will you? Me and Ryan are making a bet on whose team is going to come first in the hike. If Ryan's team beat mine then I've agreed to do our dorm's washing for the rest of term. But if my team are faster, then he gets to do it.'

The guys raised their eyebrows and looked at each other.

'Seriously?' Lee had a look of disbelief as he glanced at Ryan. 'You're agreeing to this? Are you sure?'

Ryan could hardly back down now that a small crowd had formed. Besides, he was getting more and more annoyed that everyone seemed sure he'd lose. 'Yeah. I'm confident. We're gonna win.'

'But until the end of term? That's four weeks Ryan. You'll be in the laundry room every other day!'

'Tell Kev that. He's the one who'll be doing it.' Ryan sounded a lot more confident than he felt.

'Well,' cut in Ranjit, wanting to see how this turned out, 'if you're serious then shake on it. But if you do then there's no going back on the deal, ok?'

'Sure.' Ryan offered his hand to Kev and the older lad shook it.

'You've got guts, I'll give you that.' Kev leaned back in his seat. 'But you shouldn't have made that deal. Our team came up with amazing ideas this afternoon. Lee and Mark were on fire, weren't you, Lee?'

Lee blushed bright red. 'I don't normally get ideas that fast. I'm well up for this hiking thing. I have so much energy right now!'

Ryan was feeling worse and worse. He always hated backing down. Now he was going to pay for it. It was like a part of his brain had it in for him.

At that moment, a loud cheer from the other side of the common room interrupted Ryan's thoughts. The lads all glanced over to see what was causing the commotion.

Mark—the older lad on Kev's team—was standing up grinning from ear to ear. Across from him sat Jael, his head in his hands.

'Guys, you'll never guess what!' Jason shouted over, his face flushed with excitement. 'Mark beat

Jael at chess!'

Normally, winning at chess wouldn't be a big deal, but for anyone to beat Jael was unheard of. He was a junior grandmaster and usually won every game he played.

Ryan took it as a good sign and nudged his friend. 'Hey Kev, it seems that sometimes even the underdog gets to win. I'd be afraid if I were you.'

'Yeah,' nodded Kev. 'But before you get too sure of yourself, you might want to remember that Jael is on *your* team.'

7. CRAZY

Towards the end of the evening, Ryan took one last trip to the laundry room and carried all the dry clothes back to his dorm. He dumped them on his bed and almost headed straight back out, but realised he should probably put everything away. Opening the wardrobe, he started hanging up the jackets and folding the trousers. He even paired up the socks and folded the vests and rugby shirts. When he'd finished, it looked impressive.

'*Now* tell me I never pull my weight,' he muttered to himself, heading back into the corridor. He'd just have time for a game of pool before lights out. Then he groaned as he realised he still didn't have any ideas for the hike.

In the common room, he hunted out Sparks. It wasn't difficult. The overweight cadet was sitting in his usual armchair.

'Hey, Sparks,' nodded Ryan, settling on the arm.

'Ryan! How you doing?' Sparks beamed at him as he was a long-lost friend who had returned after many years.

'I'm alright, but I need your help.' Ryan checked no-one else was listening. 'I have to come up with ideas for our team for the hike.'

Sparks put his hands up in a gesture of surrender and leaned back. 'You know I can't, mate. Everyone wants ideas right now. And my team won't thank me for sharing ours. Besides, I can't help you with your private bet. That's between you and Kev.'

'I guess so.' Ryan hadn't thought about the fact that Sparks might want to keep his ideas to himself for a change. He must have looked worried because Sparks put his hand on Ryan's knee.

'Don't worry, you'll think of something. It's not worth panicking about. It's a fun challenge, that's all.'

'Yeah, I know.'

But the hike had become this massive scary event—an ordeal which Ryan would have to share with a team that hated him. He sat in silence for a minute or two, trying to work out something he could suggest in the team meeting.

Suddenly, there was an almighty crash.

Mark Collins was standing next to an upturned coffee table, his face a picture of pure rage. He was looking from side to side, snarling like a rabid dog.

'Mark, Mark, are you ok? What's wrong?' Ayana was trying to calm him down.

Mark gave off a half-strangled yell and threw himself at the younger girl, knocking her to the ground. He got several blows in before three other cadets could grab his arms.

Mark's movements were wild. He spat in the face of one of lads who was holding him, before head-butting him. The lad cried out and let go of the older boy's arm, reaching up to cradle his bleeding nose.

With one of his arms now free, Mark punched another lad hard in his stomach, flooring him. He followed it through by kicking him several times in rapid succession. By now, the third lad had backed off, afraid.

'You're going to die. YOU'RE ALL GOING TO DIE!' Mark shrieked and gave a crazy laugh, moving towards a group of younger cadets in the corner. They were terrified, huddled near to one another, eyes wide.

'Not today, Mark,' yelled Kev, launching himself off a sofa and rugby-tackling the mad boy to the ground. 'Lads, give me some help here!'

A few cadets ran over to hold Mark down. Now he was on the floor, it was a lot easier. They soon had a person restraining each limb while Kev knelt on his torso.

'Mark, what is wrong with you?' demanded Kev. Mark was a quiet and geeky kid. Ryan couldn't recall seeing him get angry before.

Mark didn't answer. He was wriggling, hissing and spitting. His eyes narrowed and his head jerked.

'Fetch help!' shouted Kev. 'I'm not sure how long we can hold him!'

A couple of cadets darted out of the room.

Sarah Devonmoor was kneeling by the poor lad who had taken a kicking. He was lying on the floor, whimpering with pain. 'Do we have a medical specialist?' she shouted.

'Sort of.' Greg Joiner—a younger lad—ran over to

check out the wounded cadet.

The door to the common room burst open and two of Devonmoor's staff—Dr Torren and Dr Fleur—strode in, accompanied by three of the soldiers who patrolled Devonmoor at night. The soldiers wore full combat gear and carried guns; Ryan always found the sight of them disturbing.

'Situation report?' Dr Fleur looked straight at Sarah.

'Cadet Collins just went crazy, ma'am. We have two boys and one girl injured.'

Dr Torren, dressed in his immaculate grey suit and waistcoat, walked over to where Mark was being restrained and knelt down to look at the boy.

'Cadet Collins, I think it's time you had a little rest.' The teacher waved his hand in front of Mark's face. He had switched to his hypnotic voice, the one which all cadets had learned to fear. Rumour had it that Dr Torren could get anyone to do anything by using that voice and Ryan had seen him hypnotise his parents with it when he was first brought to the school. That's what had convinced them to let him stay. 'As you lay there, you must be feeling tired, so tired, and it would be such a relief to lie back and sleep. Even now you can feel yourself growing calmer, and your body drained of all its energy...'

Mark took no notice. He screamed with rage and spat at the teacher, who took out an old-fashioned handkerchief and wiped the saliva off his face.

'You can't fight it, Mark,' soothed the doctor. 'The more you try to work up your rage, the more you feel your energy ebbing away. Disappearing, like smoke in the air. Your limbs must feel so heavy as you lie there...'

But Mark could fight it, because in a sudden movement he almost kicked off the cadet holding down one of his legs. Dr Torren stood up, perplexed. Ryan had never seen the teacher fail before and it scared him. What was happening to Mark?

'I'm afraid we're going to have to do this the hard way,' Dr Torren said to his colleague as he stroked his beard.

Dr Fleur had been kneeling by the injured boy, checking if it was safe to move him to the medical room, but now she stood up and walked over, bringing the first aid kit with her. 'No problem.' Her voice betrayed no emotion. She unzipped the bag and reached inside, pulling out a fierce-looking needle and a bottle of clear fluid. 'Gentlemen, could you hold his arm?'

The soldiers pinned Mark's arm to the floor.

Dr Fleur filled the needle and flicked it, before crouching down and injecting it into the fuming cadet. The boy let off a blood-curdling howl as the needle went in, and for a few seconds it looked as if he might break free, but the soldiers held him fast.

'I think ten seconds should do the trick.' The doctor put the needle away.

Sure enough, as Ryan counted to ten in his head, Mark eased out of consciousness. After a few last convulsions, he lay still on the common room floor. The soldiers hauled Mark's unconscious body up by his arms and dragged him out.

Meanwhile, some others had been drafted in to help the injured cadets, and they walked them towards the medical room.

After so much chaos, a deathly hush descended.

'What was that?' said one boy, his voice almost a whisper. 'He turned into an animal! He was crazy!'

'Man, he's gonna get expelled for sure.'

'Did you see his eyes? What was happening?'

Kev looked exhausted as he headed over.

'Well done mate,' said Sparks, slapping him on the back. 'That was some rugby tackle!'

'Thanks.' Kev gave him a tired smile. 'But I'm worried about Mark.'

'That was truly strange,' agreed Sparks. 'I've never seen anything like it.'

'Well,' sighed Kev, 'I think that's enough drama for one night, don't you? I'm going to bed.'

***

9.52pm.

Ryan lay back on the lower bunk as the other lads changed out of their uniforms. He enjoyed the expressions of surprise when they saw the full wardrobe. 'Clean clothes! Finally!'

'This is good work, Ryan.' Kev raised his eyebrows. 'You've even folded the vests!'

'You know me: I like to do a quality job.'

'Better late than never.' Jael was in a foul mood after losing at chess. But then, Jael was never the most cheerful of people.

'I look forward to this kind of service when you lose the hike,' added Kev, a confident grin spreading across his face. 'Perhaps you could make our beds for us as well?'

Ryan threw a pillow at him. 'Don't make me come over there, Lynx-Harton.'

Kev laughed. 'Ok, I won't. But only because I don't have time to give you a full beating before lights out.'

Lee had been sitting on the bottom bunk, knees drawn up to his chest, eyes closed. Now he jumped up.

'What's up?' Ryan asked.

'I'm not sure. I feel weird: full of energy.'

'Yeah,' agreed Ryan, 'I think it will take us all a while to sleep after that business in the common room. It's been a crazy day.'

'True.' But Lee dropped to the floor and started doing press-ups.

'Whoa!' Kev almost tripped over him. 'Easy mate, what's with the work-out?'

'Just trying to tire myself out,' said Lee.

'Well I'm not sure that's gonna work.' Kev hauled himself onto the bunk above Ryan. 'You might wake yourself up even more.'

'I don't think I could be any more awake,' puffed Lee.

'Fair enough.'

'What do you guys think happened to Mark?' asked Jael, as he lay back on his bed, staring at the ceiling. 'I mean, he played the most amazing game of chess, and then he flipped like that. It's creepy.'

'He was fine when we had our team meeting,' added Kev. 'Amazing, in fact.'

'It's not the only weird thing that happened today,' Ryan pointed out. 'There was the monkey in science. It virtually bit Mr Cho's face off.'

'You don't think they're linked?' asked Kev, curious.

'Possibly.' Ryan shrugged. 'Hard to know. I don't see how they could be.'

'They did both go completely nutso.' Jael sounded thoughtful. 'Maybe it's a disease that sends you crazy?'

Kev leaned over the side of the bunk and looked down at Ryan. 'Hey, maybe you have it Ryan?'

'Why me?'

'Well, you did do the laundry today.'

'You're a funny boy.'

There was a clicking noise, and the lights went out. At ten o'clock the light to the dorms always shut off, and the doors locked.

Lee finished his press-ups and climbed into the bottom bunk in the darkness.

'Feel any better?' asked Ryan.

'Not really,' said Lee. 'I want to go for a run.'

'Save it for the hike mate,' advised Kev. 'Nothing you can do about it now, anyway.'

'True.'

After that the boys stopped talking, but Ryan could still hear Lee tossing and turning late into the night.

He couldn't sleep either. He needed ideas for his

team, else Sarah was going to skin him. But everything he came up with seemed obvious or ridiculous. He could suggest they built a raft to help them across the river, but it was hardly an amazing idea. Other than that, he wondered if they could make an aircraft, but deep down he knew that just wouldn't work. It was no good: his ideas sucked.

And even if he thought of the most amazing idea, he knew Sarah would still give him a hard time, so there wasn't much point breaking a sweat over it.

At some point he dozed off. He awoke during the night to find Lee was back out of bed, doing more press-ups. Weird as that was, Ryan was too tired to say anything. He rolled over and drifted back to sleep.

8. LAKE

Tuesday wasn't any better than Monday.

Ryan gasped for breath and tried to stay afloat as he swam towards Hannah. The sky was overcast, and the water was freezing.

They always called this 'The Lake' but it was more of a murky pond, and green algae stuck to his hair and face. His clothes weighed him down: he hadn't been able to take anything but his boots off, and it was much harder to swim when you were fully dressed.

He glanced over to see how the other teams were doing. Much better, as usual. To his left, Lee had already got hold of Kirsty and was making his way to the bank, supporting her like a professional lifeguard. On his right, Ranjit was powering through the water like he was taking part in the Olympics.

Ryan had never been the most confident swimmer, and it showed. He eventually reached Hannah, who was pretending to be unconscious in the water, and grabbed her, dragging her body back to shore. By the time they got there, Hannah was coughing and spluttering, having been pushed under the surface several times by Ryan's unusual life-saving method.

As he laid her out on the bank and tried to remember what to do next, Ryan glanced up to see Sergeant Wright towering over him.

'You're meant to be saving her life, Jacobs, not killing her.'

'Y-Y-Yes, sir. Sorry, sir.' In the pressure of the moment, Ryan's mind went blank.

'Well?' Sergeant Wright demanded. 'What are you going to do now?'

'Err, the recovery position?' Ryan looked up to the teacher with a puzzled expression.

'Jacobs, you are a liability. God help your team on the hike.'

Sarah appeared next to the sergeant, hands on hips. 'Let me guess, he failed?'

'I think we can safely say that Hannah would be dead by now,' agreed the teacher. 'I suggest you don't leave any of the life-saving to Jacobs.' Sergeant Wright stalked off, leaving Ryan kneeling there, dripping over Hannah.

'Jacobs, is there anything you can actually do?' asked Sarah, a look of contempt on her face.

'No ma'am,' sighed Ryan. 'It appears not. Would you like me to go and drown myself, ma'am?'

'Are you back-chatting me, Jacobs?'

'No, ma'am.'

'Good. Because as things stand you're in enough trouble as it is.'

Sarah nudged Hannah with her foot. 'Hannah, you can get up now. I think Jacobs has finished displaying his incompetence for the time being.'

The younger girl stood to her feet, looking relieved. Ryan followed them back to where the rest of the cadets were gathered, his teeth chattering.

They had spent the entire morning learning basic stuff about surviving on a hike: how to tie your boots properly, keeping warm, carrying out first aid, building a fire, putting up a tent, and rescuing people from drowning. It was Ryan's idea of hell.

Sergeant Wright addressed them. 'Right, cadets. That wasn't bad. Well, from most of you anyway.' He glanced sideways at Ryan and a couple of people giggled. 'In a moment you can all get warm and dry. But first, it will do you good to feel the cold, so you know why it would be a really bad idea to get your clothes wet on the hike. We also need to cover the basics of what to do in a genuine emergency. Each of you will receive a wristband with a GPS tracking device before you begin. This will allow us to trace you. You are not permitted to cut the wristband off. Teams will stay together at all times.'

The teacher reached into an army rucksack next to his feet and pulled out a steel cylinder. It was slim and long, like a heavy-duty torch or a giant firework. 'This is a rocket flare. If you get into serious difficulty or a member of your team needs urgent medical attention, then all you need to do is take out one of your flares and fire it. We will equip each team with two of these, and they are only to be used in extreme circumstances. If you fire a flare, then your team will be rescued from any location. However, you will also have brought yourself a one-way ticket to Colonel Keller's remedial teamwork classes. So I suggest that unless any of you loses a leg then you keep pressing on with the hike, ok?'

Most of the cadets nodded. A few smiled.

The sergeant held the cylinder in front of him, resting it on the palm of his hands so they could see. 'If you need to use one of these flares, you begin by removing both of the caps, like so...' He flicked off the small plastic caps at each end. They revealed one end was covered in thin metallic foil whereas the other end had a switch and plastic ring-pull. 'The foil end must be kept upright, and you must never point it at anyone. And unless you want to experience what it's like to have a firework explode in your face, then ensure you also point it away from yourself.' He held it upright but at a slight angle. 'Then you remove the ring-pull and flick this metal switch. Ready? 3, 2, 1...'

There was a bang and a flash, and something shot out of the tube at tremendous speed. The cadets glanced up to see a bright red light, burning in the sky. It seemed to stop high in the air and then drifted towards the ground.

'There will be soldiers on look-out duty throughout the hike and if they see a flare, then they will respond immediately. Do you have any questions?'

Adams put up his hand.

'Yes?'

'Are the flares waterproof, sir?'

'Good question, Adams. Not all flares are, but these are marine distress flares, so they should be.

However, it may not be a bad idea to avoid immersing them in water, just in case. We will give each team two flares in case one malfunctions. They will, after all, be your only hope of being rescued in an emergency.'

Another cadet put up their hand. 'Is there any chance they could go off by accident?'

'Not unless you puncture the steel tube itself, and I don't think there is any danger of anyone doing that. Anything else?' Sergeant Wright looked around. 'Good. It seems that you're all feeling pretty confident about the flares. Let's put it to the test. Jacobs, get out here.'

Ryan stepped forward. 'Yes, sir?'

'You have a go. Here.' The teacher passed him another of the steel tubes. 'Demonstrate to everyone how it's done. I figure if you can manage it, then anyone can.'

More smirks from the other cadets.

Firing the flare had looked simple enough, but Ryan panicked that he'd somehow get it wrong. His hands trembling, he popped the red caps off either end, and then twisted the cylinder so that the foil end was pointing towards the sky. Then he carefully removed the red plastic ring-pull and held the steel tube away from his body. He pulled the trigger further and further back, a pained expression on his face.

BANG!

The red flare flew into the sky where the other cadets watched its speedy ascent and gradual descent back to earth.

'Well done, Jacobs,' said the drill sergeant, putting his hand on Ryan's shoulder, 'though you might want to do it quicker in an actual emergency.'

Some students grinned, and a couple laughed out loud. Ryan shuffled back to his place.

'Right, you can all go. Those of you who got wet, make sure you have a long, hot shower and change into clean clothes.'

As the cadets made their way back to the academy, Sarah fell in step next to Ryan. 'Well, Jacobs, that was another rather below-average performance from you.'

'What? The flare?' Ryan had given up any hope that he'd ever meet Sarah's high standards.

'Not the flare. The entire morning.'

Ryan bit his lip and stayed silent. He'd learned the hard way what happened when you lost your temper at Devonmoor and it wasn't worth it.

'I hope that you at least have some good ideas to share with the rest of the team this afternoon. Otherwise we're going to be having words.' Sarah's voice was icy, threatening.

'Yes, ma'am.' Ryan felt his stomach tighten.

He had nothing he'd consider a particularly good idea.

They would definitely be having words.

9. LOYALTY

Just as Ryan thought the day couldn't get any worse, he remembered he needed to report to the drill hall instead of going to lunch. He stood in line alongside Kev and the other unfortunate cadets, listening to the colonel drone on.

'Day two, cadets. Remember how hungry you were yesterday afternoon?'

Ryan could remember. If it hadn't been for the chocolate bar he'd coaxed out of Mr Davids, he knew that he'd have been starving for hours.

'By now you've had time to bond with your team, and to work out if they are worth the noble sacrifice you made.' The colonel strolled up and down the line of cadets, his hands clasped together behind his back. He paused in front of Drew—the lad who had bullied Ryan in the changing rooms. Ryan had been glad to discover that Drew was on Sarrell's team for the hike, so he was probably going to be on the receiving end of some harsh treatment himself. The colonel got right up to Drew's rodent-like face as he spoke. 'But, for a few of you, the cracks will start to show. You may realise that not everyone on your team appreciates you. They are using you. Why suffer for them?' To be fair to the boy, he didn't flinch.

The colonel turned on his heel and started pacing the line again. 'So, I repeat my offer from yesterday. From this moment you have one minute to step forward. If you do so, you will go to the lunch hall and eat well, while your team are brought back here to replace you. If, however, you choose to stay where you are then you will be here for a very long time and you *will* go hungry.'

Ryan wasn't sure what to do. He knew it was a poor display of teamwork to swap places with the other members, but nothing he did seemed right as far as they were concerned, and part of him wanted to make them suffer like he had.

Just step forward! They think you're a failure anyway, so you might as well at least get some food.

The selfish part of his brain demanded action, but his body stayed where it was. Kev stood next to him; he was the sort of guy who would rather die than betray his team, and Ryan couldn't bring himself to step forward with him watching.

'Thirty seconds, cadets. Decide how you want to spend the next hour.'

One cadet stepped forward.

'Good, good,' soothed the colonel. 'You won't regret it. Anyone else? Ten seconds.'

One more stepped forward.

Join them! Your team hate you! Why would you do this for them?

'Five, last chance? Three, two, one... no, the offer has now expired. You two come with me. Everyone else, don't you dare move.' The two cadets who had accepted the offer followed the colonel. Neither looked very happy; they knew they'd let their teams down.

A short time passed and Colonel Keller returned to the drill hall with seven more people. They looked confused as they took their place standing in line.

'Welcome to those of you who have joined us,' began the colonel. 'In case you are unsure why you have been brought here, your chosen team member opted to have lunch instead of you. You, therefore, are going to spend the rest of your lunchtime here.' He waited a few seconds for the reality of that to sink in. 'This afternoon, you are all going to be meeting in your teams to finalise your project designs. I trust the fact that those individuals have *betrayed* you won't interfere with your ability to work well together?' He gave a thin-lipped smile, which didn't quite reach his eyes. 'Forty-nine minutes left, cadets. Enjoy.'

***

Ryan went straight from the drill hall to the maths classroom where his team meeting was due to take place, having checked the special timetable outside the canteen.

'Jacobs,' said Sarah, drily. 'What a pleasant surprise!'

Ryan decided not to respond, taking his place at the table in silence. Even when he did things right, she didn't lay off. Hannah was already there and Jael walked in a few moments later.

'Excellent. We can begin.' Sarah leaned back in her chair and placed her hands on the desk. 'This afternoon we need to decide what device or invention we are going to make tomorrow to help us win the hike. We have to get a design together ready for our meeting with a teacher at three-thirty. Ok?'

They all nodded.

'So, it's the moment we've all been waiting for! Cadet Jacobs, I believe you have some amazing ideas for us?'

Ryan ran his hand through his hair. 'Yeah, sure, I guess so.'

'Well?'

'Err, well I wondered about a sort of raft?' he suggested. 'There's a river we have to cross, so I figured we might make a lightweight boat.'

'Ok.' Sarah's voice was neutral. 'What kind of design are you proposing?'

'Design? I didn't get that far,' admitted Ryan. 'I just thought a raft might be a good idea.'

'Brilliant, as usual,' Jael muttered. 'Anything else? Or did it take you the whole day to come up with that?'

'I wondered about a hang-glider?'

Even Hannah raised her eyebrows at that, but these were looks of disbelief, not excitement.

'Let's get this straight,' said Sarah, icily, 'You think we should build some kind of aircraft tomorrow? For the four of us? And our luggage?'

'Yeah, well, I know it might be difficult,' admitted Ryan, 'but if we could then we'd go a lot faster than anyone else.'

'Yes, I imagine we would.' Sarah rubbed her face with both hands. 'I almost don't want to ask if you came up with anything else?'

'No,' admitted Ryan. 'Sorry.'

Sarah was quiet for a moment, probably visualising a million different ways she'd like to cause him pain. 'So that's it. A raft, which you haven't bothered to design, or an aircraft. They're your ideas.'

'Yep, pretty much.'

Sarah glanced at Jael. 'Well, you're friends with him. How would you rate these ideas on a scale of one to ten?'

'Two.' Jael looked at Ryan. 'And I don't think I'd call him my friend right now.'

'How about you, Hannah?' Sarah asked the younger girl.

'I don't know,' she muttered. 'Yesterday we said a raft was a good idea, so maybe four?'

'It's pretty pathetic,' concluded Sarah. 'You skive off the team meeting and then drift in here with ideas you came up with in the last ten minutes. You're not showing much in the way of team effort here.'

Ryan was done. Sarah had laid into him all morning. He was hungry and annoyed and couldn't handle any more criticism. He didn't deserve it. Something inside him snapped, and the rage came streaming out. He slammed his hands down on the table and stood up. 'FINE! They're bad ideas, I admit it. But whatever I came up with wouldn't be good enough for you, would it? You've got it in for me! You don't want me on this team, and I don't want to be here. So you know where you can stick your precious team! I'm out of here.'

Ryan stormed out of the classroom, slamming the door. He headed straight to the boys' toilets and locked himself in a cubicle while he tried to gather his thoughts.

He'd been determined not to lose it, not to let his temper take control of him. But there was only so much he could take, and he'd reached his limit. His team had treated him like he was trash from the start. Well, except for Hannah; she seemed ok. But Jael and Sarah would never get off his case.

But now what? There was no way he was going back. He'd get into loads of trouble for abandoning his team and Sarah would make his life more difficult. How much worse could it get?

There was only one place Ryan felt safe, one teacher he knew he could trust. Taking deep breaths to calm himself down, he left the toilets and headed straight to the computer lab.

10. CODE

The subdued blue lights and the quiet hum worked their magic on Ryan as he entered.

He could hear noise coming from Mr Davids office, so he headed over. The door was ajar, and the teacher was pacing back-and-forth muttering to himself, his desk covered in printouts of code. Behind him on a whiteboard were impressive-looking equations and strings of numbers.

'Sir?'

'Ah, Ryan, my boy. Come in, come in!' The teacher seemed pleased to see him. 'Got the afternoon off?'

'Sort of,' said Ryan. 'My team don't want my input in their planning session so I came here instead.'

It was partly true, and Mr Davids seemed to accept it. 'Well, their loss, their loss... I could certainly use your help with this.' He pointed to the whiteboard.

'Sure, sir, I'll try.'

Ryan wasn't sure he'd understand anything that was written there, but he was happy to have a go. He learned useful stuff when Mr Davids was around, so it was always worth the effort.

'Grab a seat, my boy!'

Ryan removed a pile of papers and a couple of

books from one of the soft chairs, depositing them on the floor. It was hard to move in this office without displacing something—it made Ryan's room at home look tidy.

A giant bookcase covered one wall, and the whiteboard another. There were some photos as well. In one of them Mr Davids was being awarded a special prize, and in the other he was on a protest march, holding a placard saying 'MAKE LOVE, NOT WAR'. He looked much younger, with long shoulder-length hair; the guy was an old-school hippy.

'Right,' began Mr Davids, perching on the edge of his desk next to his huge computer. 'You remember me saying there was a problem with the Chaos Flower, yes?'

'Yeah, sure. Because if a virus corrupts a system too much then it may not be possible to restore it.'

'Or so they say, so they say.' Mr Davids sucked on the end of his whiteboard marker for a moment. 'But every program corrupts data in a particular way, yes? Most computers don't do true random.'

'I guess not,' conceded Ryan. It was very difficult to get a computer to do anything by chance. They could sort of generate random numbers, but in reality they took these from a huge list in the computer's memory rather than appearing from nowhere.

'So let's approach this as if we were developing a virus. Forget the hard part—the infiltration of the computer. Let's focus on what comes next.'

'You mean the damage part?'

'Yes, yes, exactly. Here.' Mr Davids handed Ryan

a blank sheet of paper and then scrabbled around for a pen. He found one and threw it at the boy.

'Design me a level five algorithm that would freeze a computer out while corrupting its data.'

'Level five? Ok. No problem.' Ryan knew how to do that. He leaned on the coffee table in front of him and got to work, slipping off the chair and on to the floor.

After several minutes of furious scribbling, Ryan looked up. 'Ok. I'm done.'

'Good, good.' Mr Davids held his hand out for the paper and Ryan handed it to him. 'Ah, yes, a variation of the Reinbech Loop. A beautiful piece of code. And I see you added a few touches of your own, yes?'

'Of course, sir,' smiled Ryan, a little cocky. 'You know me.'

'Indeed, indeed.' Mr Davids wiped some equations off the whiteboard. He then wrote out odd letters and numbers: Ryan recognised it as simple machine code. He translated in his head, but what the teacher had written didn't seem to do anything important; it was a rather dull subroutine.

'A normal hum-drum piece of hard-drive,' commented Mr Davids, in response to Ryan's puzzled look. 'Nothing important. Just what takes up ninety percent of any computer system.'

'Fair enough.'

'So what does your code do to it, Ryan? What happens to it?' The teacher handed him a red whiteboard pen. 'Show me. Write the new data underneath.'

'By hand?' Ryan was confused.

'Yes, by hand. You can do that, can't you?'

'Yes, sir. I guess so.' Ryan got up from the floor and headed over to the whiteboard. He worked through the code, letter by letter, number by number, altering each of them.

It took a while. The figures wouldn't only get corrupted once, but repeatedly, and by the time Ryan had finished he had written over fifteen new lines. His brain hurt.

Mr Davids looked it over as he stepped back. 'Not bad, not bad. But I think the fourth digit should be a seven.'

Ryan scanned the transformations he had made and spotted the mistake. He rubbed it off and changed it. 'Ok. What now?'

'Well, now we work out how to get from the last line back to the first.'

It sounded simple enough, but Ryan knew it wasn't. In fact, over an hour and a half later they were still struggling to discover any kind of suitable formula or algorithm.

After their latest failed attempt, Ryan glanced at the clock: 4.07pm.

The rest of his team would have finished their planning session by now and would have met with a teacher to discuss what they needed for the next day. He wondered what they'd have said about why he wasn't there. He was going to get in a lot of trouble for this.

Which reminded him: it was Tuesday.

Every Tuesday at four o'clock he met Dr Torren for personal therapy. He had done since he came to the academy. He had to go.

'Sir, I just realised the time. I need to see Dr Torren.'

Mr Davids was deep in thought, studying the whiteboard. 'Hmm? Yes, yes, of course. You go. We'll finish this another time, yes?'

'Yes, sir. Sure.'

If he was honest, Ryan wasn't sure it was possible, but he didn't have time to argue. He headed out of Mr Davids office and ran up the stairs as fast as he could.

***

Ryan arrived to see the door to Dr Torren's room opening.

'Sir, I—' he started, assuming that the teacher was coming out.

But Mark Collins emerged, escorted by two soldiers. He was in a straight-jacket, all buckled up, his arms strapped tightly against his body.

'Mark!'

'Hey Ryan,' nodded the lad. He appeared to be back to his normal self.

'How you feeling?'

'Like an idiot,' said Mark. 'I don't know what happened.'

The soldiers didn't slow down for the two boys to have a conversation; they pushed Mark down the corridor.

Ryan stood against a wall to let them past. 'Where are they taking you?'

'A psych ward probably. Anyone's guess.' Mark looked over his shoulder. 'Tell the guys I'm sorry, ok? Especially those I hit.'

'Sure.' Ryan didn't know Mark that well, but he'd always found him to be a decent guy.

Dr Torren was standing by his door, watching the procession leave. He turned to Ryan. 'Ah, Cadet Jacobs. Come in.'

Ryan made his way into the counselling room. It was empty as always, apart from two leather chairs which faced each other. All the walls were painted black, and there were no pictures, just one large window looking out onto the beautiful garden at the front of the academy.

'Sir, what will happen to him? To Mark?' he asked.

'Hard to tell. He appears to be back to normal, but we can't take any risks right now. He may have another episode. We're monitoring him carefully. In time, we'll know more.'

'And until then he's going to be locked up in a straight-jacket?'

'Yes, that seems to be for the best.' Dr Torren settled in his chair. 'Take a seat.'

Ryan slumped down.

The doctor studied him for a while in silence. 'You're edgy today, Jacobs,' he stated. 'Why's that? What do you have to hide?'

'Nothing,' said Ryan. 'I'm fine.'

Dr Torren looked at him, as though he was staring

into Ryan's soul. 'You know it's pointless lying to me, Ryan. Just spit it out. What's troubling you?'

'The project, sir,' admitted Ryan. 'I'm not getting on so well with my team. I kind of stormed out of our meeting this afternoon.'

'Stormed out? In anger?'

'I guess.'

'It's been a while since you lost your temper, Jacobs.' Dr Torren's voice was neutral. 'You seemed to be getting it under control.'

'I know, sir. But Sarah winds me right up. She knows how to push all the wrong buttons.'

'Sarah Devonmoor,' mused the doctor. 'Yes, I imagine she does. Or all the right ones?'

'What does that mean?' said Ryan, confused.

'It's nothing to be ashamed of, if you find her attractive.'

'It's not like that.' Ryan clammed up.

The doctor gave a thin smile. 'Ok, let's explore something else for a while. We know that teamwork isn't one of your strong points, Jacobs.'

'No, sir. I guess not.'

'So this week is a rather special opportunity for your personal development. A great way to work out your issues.'

'Maybe,' allowed Ryan.

'So let's start with the basics. What annoys you about Sarah and the others?'

Ryan thought for a moment. 'They don't appreciate me, sir. They haven't said one positive thing to me all week. They're, like, hyper-critical.

They're always telling me I'm doing stuff wrong and shouting at me.'

'I see.' Dr Torren leaned forward. 'Do you know what projection is, Ryan?'

'No, I don't think so.'

'It's when people project all the stuff that they don't like about themselves onto other people, and then they hate those people because of it.'

'Oh.' Ryan didn't like where this was going.

'So, it's possible that you're the one who is not being very positive, who is always telling other people they're in the wrong.' Dr Torren leaned back and waited a moment. 'Is that what's happening here?'

'No.'

'Ok, well tell me a couple of positive things you've said to your teammates this week.'

Ryan thought. He thought hard. Nothing came to mind.

'Come on, Ryan,' coaxed the doctor, after a brief silence. 'There must be at least one time? You must have encouraged them about something?'

'I can't remember.' Ryan knew it sounded weak.

'Ok. So over the last two days you can't think of a single instance where you've praised anyone on your team. And yet you expect them to give positive feedback to you. Why is that?'

Ryan looked at the floor. 'I don't know, sir.'

'You also said they're always criticising you and shouting at you?'

'Yeah, you should have heard them this morning.'

'And do you ever shout at people, Ryan? For doing

things wrong?'

He was going to deny it, but then he remembered the football match and the way he'd got so frustrated with the players who were defending. 'Sometimes.'

'Well, it seems we have something then, doesn't it?' The doctor smiled. 'You're blaming everyone else for things that you hate about yourself.'

'I guess.' Ryan wasn't convinced, but he knew from bitter experience that there was little point arguing. 'So what do you suggest, sir?'

'I suggest, Jacobs, that you make a genuine effort this week to get on with your team. Give them loads of praise, encouragement and respect. Apologise for getting mad at them. Tell them you accept responsibility for being a bad team member, and that you're grateful for all their constructive criticism. Admit that the problems until now have all been down to you, but that you'll try to change.'

'You want me to say that it's all my fault?' Ryan was appalled.

'You're the only cadet who stormed out of the team meeting, I assume?'

'Yeah.'

'Then, Ryan, look at me.' Dr Torren stared into his eyes. 'It *is* all your fault. Do something about it.'

11. RAGE

Ryan was starving by the time he sat down for dinner, and he wasn't looking forward to facing his team.

'Sarah, I—' he began.

'Quiet, Jacobs,' she cut in. 'I've had enough of you for one day.'

'But I want to say that I'm sorry,' Ryan blurted out, 'and I'll make more of an effort. To be a good member of the team, I mean.'

'You want to be a good team member? Then shut up. I don't want to hear another word from you.'

Jael smirked at him and Hannah looked away.

Ryan wasn't too sure that Dr Torren's advice was working all that well, but what could he do? Maybe Sarah would warm to the apology in time. He wanted to know what his team had designed that afternoon, but he didn't want to risk annoying Sarah any more. He guessed they had no intention of telling him, anyway. They'd make him pay for storming out of their meeting.

For now, Ryan was just glad to have some food, and he was soon shovelling his way through a bowl of pasta. The day seemed so much longer when you didn't get any lunch, and Ryan hoped the colonel wouldn't repeat his drill hall exercise tomorrow.

As he ate, he noticed Lee had stood up and was making his way out the dining room. As the boy passed the teachers, Colonel Keller stepped out and blocked his path.

'Cadet Young,' demanded the colonel, 'do you have permission to leave?'

Everyone stopped talking. The colonel's voice had that kind of effect. Lee performed a few wild gestures with his hand. His body started to shake.

'Answer me, cadet.' The colonel stood in front of him, hands on hips.

Lee opened his mouth, but instead of answering, he screamed—the kind of scream you only hear in a horror film. Then he hurled himself at the colonel, fists flying. He caught the grizzled officer right in the face, and then in the stomach. They were short, sharp jabs of wild fury.

Ryan couldn't believe his eyes: hitting the colonel was suicide.

The colonel seemed just as shocked. He stood his ground, barely moving in response to the blows; his towering, heavy-set body more than able to cope with the assault from the skinny lad. He watched him for a few moments; a strange look of confusion, anger and amusement on his face. Then, with remarkable speed, he grabbed both of Lee's flailing arms, holding the boy by his wrists. 'CADET YOUNG! WHAT IS THE MEANING OF THIS?'

But Lee was no longer himself. Like Mark the night before, his face was contorted with rage and he let off another crazy shriek, bringing his knee up towards the colonel's privates. Being so much shorter, he didn't quite pull it off. Ryan was disappointed; to have seen the colonel get kicked in the balls would have been amazing.

By now, though, other members of staff came running. Sergeant Wright and Dr Torren grabbed Lee's legs from behind, and they carried the struggling boy from the canteen. Dr Fleur followed them out.

Once the teachers had left, everyone started talking.

Jael looked over at Ryan, the code of silence on their table broken. 'What was that about?' he asked, worried.

'No idea.' Ryan's stomach was in knots. Lee was his closest friend.

'What do you think they'll do to him?' asked Jael.

'I think he'll be ok. I saw Mark earlier,' admitted Ryan. 'He seems to have recovered fine. But they're keeping him under observation, whatever that means.'

'It means locked up.'

'Pretty much. They're worried he'll have another fit.'

'Let's hope not. Let's hope they're both ok. But even if Lee recovers, what then? The colonel is going to kill him.' Jael looked at Ryan, thinking through the implications. 'He'll be the colonel's whipping boy.'

'True.'

Jael was right: Lee had dug his own grave. There

was no way the colonel would pass up on the opportunity to make an example of him. For weeks to come.

Lee.

The kindest lad at the academy.

It didn't seem fair.

'He was acting strange last night.' Jael was thinking out loud. 'He kept saying he was full of energy and couldn't sleep.'

Ryan remembered waking up to find him doing press-ups in the early hours. 'I thought he was just wired about this hiking thing.'

'It's like a virus that sends people mad,' suggested Jael.

Ryan thought back to the events in the science lab at the start of the week. 'Maybe we all got it from that monkey. Lee got scratched by it.'

'That's true.' Jael frowned. 'But Mark wasn't there. He was in a different lesson.'

'Well, they could have all got it somewhere else. The monkey, Mark and Lee could have caught it from the same carrier?'

'Could be.'

They resumed eating in silence, working through the possibilities. Whatever was going on, it had sent two lads crazy in as many days. Ryan glanced around.

He wondered who would be next.

***

9.43pm.

The dormitory seemed empty without Lee. All three lads had left the common room early. Everyone had been discussing what had happened: to Lee, to Mark, to the monkey.

The disease had a name now. They were calling it 'The Fury'. One lad suggested making a bet on who got it next. At that point, the boys headed back to their dorm before Kev got mad enough to punch him.

Ryan sat on the bed in his vest, boxers and socks while Kev paced up and down the middle of the dormitory. Ryan had never seen him so worked up.

'I don't understand why people don't get it. Why are they joking about it? Lee could get expelled! And Mark! No-one knows if they're going to be ok, or if anyone else is gonna get ill!'

The others didn't respond. Kev wasn't angry with them; he just needed to get it out of his system.

BANG!

Without warning, the door to the dorm flew open and Sergeant Wright stormed in with two soldiers. One of them had a dog.

'Against the wall, cadets,' he ordered.

'Sir?'

The lads froze, unsure what was happening.

'Are you deaf? I said AGAINST THE WALL! NOW!'

They didn't need telling again.

Sergeant Wright and the soldiers started ripping all the sheets off their beds, turning over the mattresses, and pulling clothes out of the wardrobe. They were searching the dormitory. The dog—a huge Alsatian—

sniffed around.

'Turn around, hands on the wall,' ordered the other soldier, walking over to the lads. He searched them, ensuring nothing was hidden in their clothing.

Ryan felt violated, standing against the wall in his underwear. 'You enjoying that?' he muttered to the soldier.

'Quiet, Jacobs,' cut in Sergeant Wright. 'One more word from you and I'll have you digging ditches for a week.'

Ryan shut up. It wasn't worth the risk.

'There's nothing here, sir,' said the soldier with the dog, after a few minutes.

There was a brief pause.

Sergeant Wright approached the boys. 'Where are they?' he asked.

'Where are what, sir?' asked Kev, confused.

'The drugs, cadet.'

No-one said anything for a few seconds. They hadn't considered the possibility that Lee and Mark could have been taking drugs. It was impossible to get anything like that onto the Devonmoor campus.

'There aren't any, sir,' said Ryan. 'Lee would never do drugs.'

Sergeant Wright was in a foul mood and he walked right up to Ryan, staring him down. 'Well then, Cadet Jacobs. Perhaps you know what else could have caused that little outburst in the dining room?'

'No, sir,' admitted Ryan. He glanced at the others, hesitating. 'We wondered if it might be a virus?' He couldn't see any reason not to tell the sergeant. It seemed a lot more likely than drugs.

'A virus? Like the crazy flu?' Sergeant Wright was not convinced. 'Do you know many viruses that cause that kind of reaction, Jacobs?'

'No, sir.' Ryan wished he'd kept his mouth shut.

'I didn't hear you, Jacobs.'

'NO, SIR.'

The sergeant backed off a little. He turned to one of the soldiers. 'Fetch Dr Torren. Now.'

The soldier headed off down the corridor.

'You know what happens now, boys,' stated Sergeant Wright. 'The doctor will find out anything you know. So, I'm going to give you one last opportunity to come clean, before things get any more serious than they already are. Anyone?'

No-one spoke.

'Fine. Have it your way.'

The next five minutes dragged, the boys standing against the wall like criminals while the sergeant checked and double-checked the room for a hidden drugs stash. It was in a proper state by now: the mattresses turfed onto their sides, the bedding and clothes all over the floor. Ryan was annoyed that all his careful work putting the clean clothes away had been ruined.

Eventually, Dr Torren strode in.

'Ah, doctor.' The sergeant greeted him. 'Sorry to call on you so late but I need you to find out if these boys know anything about drugs.'

'Yes, an important question,' agreed Dr Torren. 'Turn around and face me, cadets.' Kev, Ryan and

Jael swivelled round. 'Did any of you have any suspicions at all that Cadet Young was taking drugs?'

'None at all,' replied Kev.

'That's because he wasn't,' added Ryan. 'Lee didn't take anything.'

'How about Collins? Was he on drugs?'

'No, sir,' answered Kev. 'Not as far as I know.'

'Neither Mark nor Lee would do anything like that,' added Jael.

The doctor seemed satisfied. He turned to Sergeant Wright. 'What can I say? They believe what they're telling us. There's not a trace of deception here. They don't know anything about it.'

That wasn't what Sergeant Wright wanted to hear, but he thanked the doctor, who left.

The sergeant glowered at the three cadets. 'Don't think I'm not onto you. You might be able to act all innocent with Dr Torren, but this isn't over. You have four minutes until lights out. I suggest you clean up in here.' With that he stalked out of the room, followed by the soldiers and the dog.

The boys surveyed the damage.

'Drugs?' said Jael. 'They think they were taking drugs?'

'It's crazy,' agreed Kev. 'I can't see Lee on drugs, can you?'

Ryan smiled. Kev was right. The whole idea was absurd.

'Besides, how would he get hold of them,' pointed out Jael.

Kev sorted through the clothes on the floor, trying

to work out what was clean and what wasn't. Ryan knelt down to help him. A few minutes later, the lights went out.

'That's all we need,' sighed Kev.

The lads had to finish the job in the dark, aided only by the small light from the bathroom in the corner. Ryan didn't know how long it took them, but by the time he fell into bed, he was shattered.

'Hey Kev?' he said, quietly.

'Yeah? What?'

'If you do have drugs, you will share them with us, won't you? I could use some this week.'

'Yeah,' Kev said, chuckling. 'Me too.'

12. REJECTED

Sergeant Wright had it in for them at drill the next morning. Ryan wasn't sure why, but he guessed the instructor still suspected the lads knew something about the Fury that they weren't telling.

'Lynx-Harton,' he said, standing in front of Kev, 'did you decide to try out a new hairstyle this morning?'

'No, sir.'

Ryan risked a quick glance over. Kev's hair looked as neat as it always did.

'Well perhaps you could at least try brushing it before you come to drill in the future?' suggested the sergeant, 'or I will personally shave it all off.'

'Yes, sir.'

'Give me thirty press-ups cadet.'

Kev knuckled down to do as he was told, and the sergeant headed further along the line, stopping by Jael, looking him up and down. Jael was always immaculate: he polished his boots every night and had an obsessive-compulsive approach to his uniform.

The sergeant struggled to find anything he could criticise. 'Stand straighter, Marquez. Don't slouch.'

Jael tightened his chest and thrust his chin a little higher, lifting his shoulders up as he did so.

'Better.' Wright now strolled down the next line, heading straight for Ryan. 'Jacobs?'

'Yes, sir.'

'The colonel has asked to see you in his office straight after drill. He didn't sound too happy, so I suggest you don't keep him waiting.'

'Yes, sir.'

At least the message seemed to prevent the sergeant from needing to find something wrong with his uniform. Grateful as Ryan was for that, he wondered what the colonel wanted.

Whatever it was, it wouldn't be good.

***

Despite having had more than his fair share of dealings with Colonel Keller, Ryan had never been summoned to his office before. It was a short distance from Lady Devonmoor's room, and he looked longingly towards the other door, knowing the elderly headteacher would offer him tea and biscuits and a friendly chat; he doubted very much that's what he was going to experience here.

He knocked.

'Enter.'

Ryan turned the handle and made his way inside. The room was pretty much what he'd expected.

The colonel sat in a leather chair behind an enormous oak desk that filled most of the space.

Behind him was a trophy cabinet, displaying various medals, photos and awards. Everything was immaculate: the desk was empty except for a computer screen in one corner and a lamp in the other—the kind that lawyers use. A large window on Ryan's left stood open, allowing in a gentle breeze. There was plenty of daylight, but the room stood in the academy's shadow. On Ryan's side of the desk were a couple of small chairs. They didn't look comfortable.

Ryan stood to attention and saluted.

The colonel leaned back on his chair and propped his heavy-booted feet up on the desk in front of him. 'At ease, Jacobs. How is our resident criminal today?'

Even a month in to Ryan's time at the academy, the colonel wouldn't let go of the fact that they had caught him hacking into the army database. As far as Colonel Keller was concerned, Ryan should be rotting in a young offenders' institution.

'Fine, sir.'

'You're here because I've been hearing reports, Jacobs.' The colonel gave a sly smile. 'These reports suggest you haven't been pulling your weight in the team activity. In fact, the other members of your team have made an official complaint about you. They want you off their team.'

Ryan tensed, but he kept his expression neutral and stayed silent. He hadn't been asked a question, so he didn't need to respond.

'This is what happens when we allow boys like you into a school like this.' The colonel was enjoying the moment. 'You can wear the uniform along with everyone else, and you can pretend that you're a Devonmoor cadet, but underneath it all, you're scum. Do you realise that you're the only person—*the only person*—that has been rejected by their own team? Does that feel good, Jacobs?'

'No, sir.'

'So,' continued the colonel, taking his feet off the desk and leaning forward. 'I've decided to let your team dump you. They reckon they would be better off without you, and I couldn't agree more. But the question is what to do with you now. You see, I can't help thinking this was part of your plan all along: miss your team meetings, get your team to kick you out, and then somehow escape having to do the hike. A typical lazy attempt to skive hard work and exercise. Is that what you had in mind?'

'No, sir. I want to do the hike.' It was partly true. The hike might be fun if he was on a decent team. Besides, if he didn't do it then he'd lose the bet with Kev. 'Please give me another chance.'

'Your team don't want you, Jacobs. I could force them to take you back, but why would I?'

'Then assign me to a different team, sir. Any team. And I'll prove to you I can do this. What do you have to lose?'

The colonel smiled. 'I have decided to do that. But not because you deserve it. Only because I don't see why you should escape hiking thirty miles *before* you attend my remedial teamwork classes.'

Ryan's heart sank. 'Is there no way out of the extra

classes now, sir?'

'Theoretically, yes.' There was an evil glint in Colonel Keller's eye. 'If your new team are the first back, and they have no complaints, then I'll think about letting you off. Otherwise, say goodbye to your weekends.'

'Yes, sir,' Ryan said miserably. Both things seemed unlikely, but if he ended up on a good team, then at least they weren't impossible.

'I will interview your team leader after the hike, and I expect a glowing report from them. I want to hear that you pulled your weight, stayed positive, did as you were told and put in a hundred and ten percent effort. In short, I need to know that you weren't the whiney, snivelling brat that you usually are. Is that clear?'

'Yes, sir. Who's my new team leader, sir?' Ryan held his breath, hoping to hear the words: *Cadet Lynx-Harton.*

He should have known better.

'I have assigned you to Cadet Sarrell.'

Ryan felt weak and dizzy, as if he'd been kicked in the head. 'Sarrell, sir? You know he hates me?'

It was a stupid question. Of course the colonel knew that. He knew exactly what he was doing. Ryan had walked straight into his trap. 'I believe you asked to be assigned to *any* other team, Jacobs? Are you suggesting that you *already* have a problem with your new team?'

'No, sir. No problem.'

No problem other than that Sarrell is going to

destroy me.

'Good.' The colonel locked eyes with Ryan. 'Be sure of one thing. If you mess up the golden opportunity I'm giving you here, then you will regret it. Sarrell is waiting for you in the engineering department. I suggest you head straight there.

***

The engineering block was a small warehouse, hidden among the trees. It looked out of place in the neat grounds of Devonmoor Academy. The inside was a vast space, roofed with corrugated iron and full of loud noises, enormous machines and the ever-present smell of oil.

As Ryan entered, he bumped into Mr McAllister: a big, burly man with long, straggly hair who spent most of his time working on crazy inventions.

'RYAN! WHAT ARE YOU DOING HERE?' shouted the teacher, over the sound of a screeching drill.

'I'M LOOKING FOR CADET SARRELL. HAVE YOU SEEN HIM?'

'OVER THERE.' Mr McAllister pointed to a small meeting room in the far corner, separated from the workspace by large double-glazed windows. Three cadets were inside, and as Ryan got closer to the room, he could make out the shaved head and tall, tough figure of James Sarrell, slouched in a chair. Opposite him was Stone, a quiet older lad, who always seemed a little cold and calculating. Then, to top it off, there was Drew—the younger rodent-faced boy who had humiliated Ryan. It was as if someone had put together a team of all the worst people at the academy. He took a deep breath and walked in.

'Morning, Jacobs.' Sarrell chewed as he spoke. 'It's good to have you on the team.'

Ryan decided to be honest from the start. 'Look, I know you don't want me here, but it seems we're all stuck with each other, so we need to make the best of it.'

'But we *do* want you here,' laughed Sarrell. 'Colonel Keller was clear about how much of a challenge you would be to work with, but you know us: we love a challenge. Right, boys?'

Stone and Drew nodded, the younger boy grinning at Ryan's misfortune.

Sarrell pulled out a notebook and placed it on the desk. 'So,' he explained. 'I'm keeping a record of everything you do wrong from now on. Every time you disobey an order, or whine, or make a negative comment, or don't pull your weight. And at the end of the week, the list gets given to the colonel. Any problem with that?'

'No,' replied Ryan, sitting down. 'We both know how this is going to work. You're gonna make my life hell but there's nothing I can do about it. Let's get on with it.'

Sarrell narrowed his eyes and smiled. 'It's good to know that we're on the same page.'

The older cadet nodded to Stone, who opened a folder in front of him and handed a sheet of paper to

Ryan. It was a rough blueprint for an all-terrain buggy. Well, more of a trolley, because it didn't have an engine and was designed to be pushed.

'That's what we're building for the hike,' explained Stone. 'To hold all our baggage.'

'Ok, good idea.' Ryan tried to sound positive. He didn't know if it would work or not but he could hardly criticise the plan.

'And it will be you who's pushing it,' added Sarrell, 'so it seems fair that you're also the one to build it.'

'What?' exclaimed Ryan. 'On my own?'

'I don't see why not. We could all use a day to chill out before the hike. Unless that's a problem?' Sarrell opened the notebook and held up a pen.

Ryan was cornered. 'No, no problem.'

'See, lads,' exclaimed Sarrell. 'I knew it was a good idea to have him on the team. It's like having our own personal slave.'

Stone grinned and pointed to a pile of scrap metal and vehicle parts lying in the corner. 'All the materials you need are over there. The buggy needs to be finished by lights out this evening. So, that gives you about twelve hours.'

'No shoddy work though, Jacobs,' added Sarrell. 'We intend to win this thing.'

The lads got up and headed to the door, Drew smacking the back of Ryan's head as he walked past.

'I will check on you later,' warned Sarrell. 'Don't disappoint me, now, will you?'

Ryan gulped. 'I'll try not to. I'll do my best.'

And to be fair, he meant it.

But as he stared at the complicated diagram, he knew for a fact that this was not going to end well.

13. LONER

Ryan swore, threw down the safety goggles and hurled the piece of metal tubing into a corner. The engineering block was empty so no-one was watching as he threw his fourth tantrum of the day. No matter how carefully he tried to use the machinery, nothing seemed to go right. Drilling holes into the metal pipes was far from simple, and they kept ending up in the wrong places. The frame for the buggy would never fit together. He'd already wasted more than half his time.

Come on, Ryan, you can do this.

The evidence suggested otherwise. So far only two metal pipes had been secured. Everything else was in a worse state than when he'd first picked it up.

That wasn't because he was slacking. Other than a quick break for lunch, he'd been hard at it, determined to get the buggy finished. He needed to impress his team, or at least to keep them off his back. But he sucked at engineering.

His frustration had built to such a level that he knew he couldn't go on any longer. He decided to take a break, to calm down.

Besides, he was desperate to find out what had

happened to Lee. He figured that if he made his way to the medical room, he might find something out. It was worth a shot.

Ryan threw all the materials for the buggy back onto one messy pile before heading outside.

***

He moved quietly through the school, grateful that the corridors were deserted. Most of the students were working hard on their projects.

As he was about to turn a corner, he heard two teachers talking. He recognised the voices: Colonel Keller and Lady Devonmoor. They were coming towards him. He wasn't sure if the corridor leading to the medical room was out of bounds but he didn't want to be seen, just in case. Fortunately, he was right by the door of an empty classroom, so he slipped inside, leaving the door ajar so he'd know when the teachers had passed.

He could make out the colonel's words as they approached: 'They should be expelled without appeal. There's no other option.'

'I would agree with you, Colonel,' said Lady Devonmoor. 'However, Cadet Young acted completely out of character. He has never so much as talked back to a teacher before. And he's the second boy in as many days to fly into a wild rage like that.'

'But we can't allow any boy to hit a teacher!'

Lady Devonmoor was doing her best to calm

Colonel Keller down. 'We will get to the bottom of this,' she said. 'And if we discover these cadets are to blame for their behaviour, then I will allow you to come up with whatever punishment you feel is appropriate. But first, we need to find out what's going on. I believe that there has to be a reason two of our nicest cadets would behave so appallingly.'

'The drugs test came back negative.' The colonel's voice was hard. 'So what else could it be? You think the Outlier is behind this? It's just the kind of thing he'd do.'

'I don't know, Julius,' admitted the headteacher. 'It's possible, but I just don't know. I do, however, intend to find out.'

***

Ryan waited for a few minutes before sneaking back out of the classroom. He was relieved to find the door to the medical room wasn't locked, and he slipped inside.

Two of the beds were occupied. Lee was lying on one of them, huge foam straps holding him down. He wasn't moving but his eyes were open and he was staring at the ceiling. Mark Collins was also there, out of the straight-jacket and sitting with some textbooks on his lap. He looked up as Ryan came in.

'Ryan!' He sounded pleased to have a visitor. 'It's good to see you! Are you allowed to be in here?'

'No idea,' admitted Ryan. Then he pointed at Lee. 'How is he?'

'I'm fine,' Lee interrupted, shifting his head to look in Ryan's direction. 'I'm just bored out of my mind.'

'Yeah, well at least you have me in here,' Mark reminded him. 'I had a day strapped up on my own. That was *after* they let me out of the cell.'

'How long will they keep you like that?' Ryan asked.

'Strapped up until this evening, and then they'll release me if there are no signs of another fit. But they'll keep me for observation for a few days after that.'

'Standard procedure,' added Mark.

'And you're fine now?' Ryan looked to both of them for an answer.

'Yeah, I feel great,' said Mark.

'Well, I wouldn't go that far.' Lee seemed depressed. 'I hit a teacher, Ryan. I don't know what I was thinking. I messed up big time.'

'I don't think you were to blame,' Ryan tried to reassure him. 'Everyone knows something weird is going on.'

'Even so,' said Lee, 'I lost control.'

'Well, Sergeant Wright thinks you're on drugs.'

'Seriously?' Lee let out a short laugh. 'Where would I get drugs from?'

'Come on, Lee. This is the sergeant. He doesn't think about stuff like that! He searched our room.'

'Does anyone have any idea what did cause it? For real?' Mark was interested.

'No. I think the teachers suspect the Outlier might be behind it—you know, the former student who hates Devonmoor. But no-one's sure. They're calling it the Fury.'

Lee groaned. 'Whatever caused it, the colonel's gonna kill me when I get out of here. My life is over. I'm gonna be doing push-ups until I puke.'

'I think we're both going to have a lot of explaining to do,' sighed Mark. 'Torren showed me the footage from the common room.'

'Did he suggest anything?' asked Ryan. Dr Torren usually had a theory.

'No, he has no clue.'

The door burst open and Dr Fleur marched in. She was surprised to see Ryan standing there. 'Cadet Jacobs,' she said. 'I'm assuming you have special permission to be here?'

'No ma'am. Sorry. I was worried about Lee.' Ryan looked at the floor.

'Well, if I catch you in here again then *he* will have good reason to be worried about *you*. Do I make myself clear?'

'Yes, ma'am.'

'Get out, Jacobs.'

Ryan fled back to the engineering block. He was grateful that the teacher hadn't given him a detention, and he was also glad that Lee was on the mend.

But something weird was going on at the academy. Even the teachers didn't know whether this was a sinister plot or if something else was causing the Fury.

Whatever it was, he was determined to find out.

14. HELP

A few hours later, Ryan was kneeling on the hard floor, trying to attach two pieces of metal tubing.

'Come on, come on...' he muttered, forcing a bolt through a hole.

It wasn't going well. The rickety collection of metal pipes which formed the frame of the buggy was nowhere near sturdy enough. He hoped that once all the other pieces were in place, it would somehow tighten up. But deep down, he knew it was a waste of time. The whole buggy project was doomed.

He was so engrossed in what he was doing that he didn't hear footsteps approaching. Ryan looked up too late, as Sarrell snatched the frame from his hands.

'*WHAT* do you call that, Jacobs?'

Drew and Stone stood behind him, sneering.

'I hope this isn't all you've accomplished in the last eight hours?' Sarrell cocked his head to one side, holding up the flimsy metal.

'Afraid so.' Ryan couldn't see any point denying it.

Sarrell grabbed two of the metal poles and levered them away from one another. The metal twisted and buckled under the pressure and one bolt broke off, allowing a piece to fall to the floor. He threw the mangled metalwork aside and walked closer to Ryan, holding his jacket, their faces close.

'Perhaps I didn't make myself clear before, Jacobs?' he hissed into Ryan's ear. 'Your life is going to get very difficult if that buggy isn't finished by lights out.'

'I'm doing my best!' exclaimed Ryan, frustrated. 'I can't do it on my own; I need help.'

'That's *not* going to happen.' Sarrell let go of Ryan and stepped back. 'You will do it by yourself. And it had better be ready when we come back.'

Ryan shook his head. 'I don't have enough time.'

Sarrell took out his notebook and a pen and started scribbling.

'Wait, what are you writing?' asked Ryan, worried.

'Negativity. Whining. Excuses. Want to add anything?' Sarrell smirked at him.

'I'm not being negative. I can't do it!'

Sarrell started writing again.

'Ok, ok. I'll try. I'm trying, ok? But I think it would be quicker if I had help.'

'So you're challenging my decision as team leader?' Sarrell raised his eyebrows.

'No,' insisted Ryan. 'No, I'm not. You're right. I'll finish it alone.'

'You'd better.'

Sarrell pocketed the notebook and strode out the engineering block, the others following. Drew spat and kicked at the wreckage as he went past, sending it skidding across the floor.

'Nice work, Jacobs,' he muttered.

Once they'd left, Ryan retrieved the damaged frame. It hadn't looked that great to start with. Now it was even worse; a mass of bent metal and broken poles.

He felt angry and exhausted. As he stood there, a sudden wave of emotion flooded over him and he crumpled to the floor, hot tears running down his cheeks.

You're a failure, Ryan. You can't do anything right.

No-one wanted to work with him, and no-one wanted him on their team. He sat there, feeling hollow inside. Right now, he needed a friend.

'Ryan?' The voice made him start. He looked up to see the large outline of Kelvin Sparks standing over him, concern on his chubby face. 'What's up mate?'

Ryan wiped his eyes with his sleeve and then gestured at the spider's web of metal tubing. 'That,' he said. 'That's up. I have to finish it by lights out, or Sarrell's gonna kill me.'

'Ah.' Sparks picked a piece up. 'Err, no offence, but what's it meant to be?'

'A buggy. See the problem?'

'A buggy?' Sparks examined it. 'Really?'

'Really.' Ryan pointed to the desk. 'The plan's over there.'

Sparks waddled over to the workbench and picked up the sketch. 'Oh, right! I see! Yep... so that goes there... and then... you need to add some kind of suspension...'

'The suspension is the last of my worries,' said

Ryan. 'At the moment it doesn't even have wheels. Or much of a frame.'

'Well,' stated Sparks, 'in that case, we'd better get a move on.'

'We?' asked Ryan, confused. He pushed himself up from the floor.

'Yep. You're never gonna finish this on your own.'

'But what happened to us being on opposite teams and not being able to help each other and stuff?'

'Look,' said Sparks, 'I shouldn't get involved, but you're a mate and I know what Sarrell's like.'

'I do love you Sparks,' grinned Ryan, wiping his nose on his sleeve.

'Besides,' said Sparks, with a twinkle in his eye, 'your team is never gonna win with this contraption, however well you make it.'

'True.'

Ryan didn't care about that any more—he just wanted Sarrell and the others off his back.

***

No kid at the academy—or probably in the country—was as good at engineering as Kelvin Sparks, who was recruited to Devonmoor after winning several competitions with his home-made fighting robots. Rumour had it he was involved in designing a craft for the European Space Agency.

For Sparks, knocking together a basic buggy was child's play. Within half an hour, he'd welded the frame of the buggy and it was solid. After that, all the wheels had been attached, along with an improved suspension system for covering unstable ground. Then a lightweight crate was added to the top for the bags to be placed into.

It looked perfect.

'Now you're sure you don't want me to add an engine?' asked Sparks, looking at the finished masterpiece.

'No mate,' smiled Ryan. 'I think they'll be suspicious enough as it is, don't you?'

'Fair enough. Well don't worry. My lips are sealed. I'm off to the common room.'

'Sparks,' said Ryan, as his friend headed out.

Sparks paused and looked back.

'Thanks. I owe you one.'

'Yep,' replied Sparks, with a wink. 'You do. Don't you forget it.'

***

Ryan enjoyed seeing the shocked looks on his team's faces when they returned to the engineering block later that evening to see how badly he'd failed. He was propped up on the workbench, swinging his legs, a broad smile on his face.

'So, guys, what do you think?'

They didn't respond at first. Sarrell walked around the buggy, pushing and prodding it at various points, lifting it to check its weight.

'It's not bad,' he admitted.

Drew scowled at Ryan, disappointed that he'd

finished.

Ryan decided to rub it in. 'Do you like it, Drew?'

The wiry kid stared at Ryan, almost hissing his reply. 'It's ok I suppose. Took long enough.' But then Drew looked eagerly towards Sarrell. 'So, are we gonna tell him now?'

'Tell me what?' asked Ryan.

Sarrell pulled up a nearby chair and sat down, his legs either side of the backrest. 'The thing is, Jacobs,' he said, 'we're not taking the buggy with us on the hike.'

'WHAT?' Ryan jumped off the workbench. 'What do you mean? I've worked on that all day!'

Drew laughed out loud—a mocking laugh—as Ryan's face turned red.

'We're not taking it, because we have something else designed,' Sarrell explained. 'We were hardly going to trust the team's success to a whining little brat like you, now were we?'

Ryan's brain was working at a million miles an hour, trying to figure out what had happened. 'So why'd you want me to build the buggy?'

'Well, that's the joy of it.' Sarrell stood up and walked closer to Ryan. 'We came up with that because we thought it would be fun to leave you slaving away in here all day. View it as a test of your loyalty to the team.'

Ryan was so close to Sarrell that he was tempted to swing his fist at the older cadet's jaw and knock his teeth out, but hitting Sarrell would be stupid and he couldn't afford to make any mistakes right now. He stayed silent, his jaw clenched.

'Nothing to say, Jacobs?' Sarrell placed a heavy, threatening hand on Ryan's shoulder. 'Not even a little whine? I'm almost disappointed.'

'I think he's angry,' sneered Drew.

'Maybe he's got the Fury?' suggested Stone, with a wry smile.

'I'm not angry.' Ryan had to force the words out through gritted teeth, willing himself to believe them. 'But if we're not using the buggy, then what? What *are* we taking?'

'You'll find out tomorrow.' Sarrell glanced sideways at Drew and a knowing look passed between them. 'And I suggest you get as much sleep as you can. You're gonna need it.'

15. TOXIC

Two coaches waited on the gravel driveway. Cadets stood in lines on the lawn, wearing their usual academy uniform. As their names were called, they marched forward.

'Collins.'

Ryan was surprised to hear Sergeant Wright shouting for Mark, but he was there, out of the medical room. They'd obviously decided that he had recovered enough to be allowed to do the hike. That was good news. It meant that Lee may also be released soon.

Hopefully, all the madness related to the Fury was over. There had been no signs of it since Lee's outburst.

'Lynx-Harton.'

Kev made his way up to the coach, following Mark inside. Ryan groaned as he realised they were being sat with their teams. He was going to have to cope with Sarrell and the others for the entire journey. It could be hours.

Sure enough, a few minutes later he found himself trapped on a seat between Drew and the window. Sarrell and Stone sat behind them.

Ryan decided he might as well try to be friendly. 'Hey.'

Drew didn't respond. He fidgeted in his seat and stared straight ahead, ignoring Ryan completely.

It didn't take many minutes for all the cadets to take their places and the coach started moving.

Ryan pressed on, figuring it would be a good plan to break the ice with Drew, even if it was hard work. 'Look,' he said. 'I've been thinking and I realise I was selfish in the football match. And I want to say sorry. Properly, I mean.'

Drew turned and looked at him with narrow eyes. 'Sure you're not just scared about what we're gonna do to you on the hike?'

What we're gonna do to you... That didn't sound good.

'Maybe a little,' admitted Ryan. 'But it's got to be best for everyone if we're getting on with each other. We're more likely to win.'

Drew shrugged. 'Makes no difference to me.'

Ryan gave up. He didn't know what else to say. He tried to relax and grab a few extra hours sleep during the journey but Drew kept fidgeting. The boy wouldn't sit still.

'Are you ok?' asked Ryan.

'Don't worry about me,' said Drew. 'I'm well up for this.'

Ryan hoped that now they were on their way, his team might at least give him a clue what their strategy was. 'I don't suppose you could let me in on the plan now?'

'Dream on, Jacobs,' smirked Drew. 'But just so you know, these could be the hardest days of your life. Ever.'

Ryan knew Drew was trying to scare him.

But it was working.

***

The coach journey dragged on into the afternoon. Ryan longed for some music, or a movie to watch, or anything to distract him as he sat there. Instead, he grew increasingly anxious about what lay ahead. Sarrell was bad enough at school, where there were teachers and other students; Ryan didn't want to think how dangerous he could be out in the wild.

He tried to think about something else.

Anything else.

All the time, Drew kept moving, elbowing Ryan. It was probably accidental, but either way, Ryan wasn't going to make a big deal out of it.

Eventually, and much to everyone's relief, the coach pulled into a military base, way out in the countryside. Once through the main gates, it stopped, and the cadets filed out.

Ryan looked at the bleak surroundings. Grassy fields and hills surrounded the car park. A couple of dull-looking buildings stood nearby. Other than the couple of soldiers they had seen at the main gate, Ryan wasn't sure if there was anyone else there. The sky was grey, but at least it didn't look like it was going to rain.

'Toilets are over there!' shouted Sergeant Wright, pointing at the nearest building. 'I suggest you make use of them and stretch your legs. We'll be dropping you at your starting points in half an hour.'

Dutifully, the cadets filtered towards the toilet block. Ryan stood in the queue next to Kev.

'Hey,' said the older boy. 'Ready to lose the bet?'

'Sure. We'll see.' Ryan's stomach sank a little as he remembered the forfeit. 'I see you got Mark back.'

'Yeah,' replied Kev. 'Otherwise, with Lee out of action, it would have just been me and Kirsty. So I spoke to the colonel, and he agreed.'

'Fair play.'

'Well, good luck,' said Kev. 'May the best team win!'

When Ryan emerged from the toilets, he was surprised to see several jeeps had arrived and were parked nearby. Next to each one stood a soldier. The cadets were taking large camouflage rucksacks from the luggage compartments of the coaches and making their way across.

Ryan did the same, grabbing a bag from the hold. He dragged it over to where Drew, Sarrell and Stone stood chatting. It was going to be pretty difficult to walk with it for any distance.

'Jacobs looks knackered already,' smirked Drew.

'Come on, Jacobs!' Sarrell aimed a harsh kick at Ryan's backside as he dumped the bag into the back of the jeep. 'You better go quicker than that!'

'Sure,' mumbled Ryan. 'Sorry.'

It wasn't many minutes until all the cadets were

accounted for. A signal passed between the soldiers.

'Climb in, boys,' ordered their driver, and he started up the engine.

***

The jeep stopped on a dirt track in the middle of nowhere. They'd parted company with the other cars some time ago and there was no-one else in sight.

'Here's your starting point,' said the soldier, climbing out and helping them unload their bags. 'The hike starts in fifteen minutes. If there's anything you don't want to take with you, then you need to leave it with me.'

Sarrell opened his rucksack and started pulling items out. Drew and Stone did the same. They created two piles of stuff, but Ryan couldn't work out the logic. He hesitated, looking down at his bag, unsure what to do.

'Hand it over, Jacobs,' ordered Sarrell, grabbing it from him. He turned it upside down, spilling the contents on the ground. He picked out the spare pair of academy-issue long grey socks and threw them at Ryan.

'Put these on, now. Over the ones you're wearing. And give me your jacket.'

Ryan reluctantly handed his jacket to Sarrell, shivering in the cold air. It was November; surely he wasn't going to do the whole hike in his vest? He wanted to say something, but knew he'd only get mocked. Besides, the other lads had taken their jackets off too, so this wasn't some kind of punishment they'd designed for him. It must be part of the plan.

He sat down and pulled off his boots. He watched as Sarrell separated out the items from his bag. The roll mat, sleeping bag, tent, water bottle, spare underwear and waterproofs all got thrown to one side. Then the torch, whistle and a couple of other items were placed back into the bag, along with Ryan's jacket and a few packets of food.

'We won't need any of this,' Sarrell said to the soldier, pointing at the stuff on the ground.

'No tent or sleeping bag?' exclaimed Ryan. 'Are you crazy? Where will we sleep?'

'We won't.' Sarrell stated. 'We keep going until we finish. We walk fast. We take the minimum amount and have a couple of rest breaks, but that's all. That way we're bound to finish first.'

'Is that possible?'

'Let's hope so.' Sarrell gave a wicked grin.

'But we'll still need the water,' pointed out Ryan.

'No we won't,' said Drew. He reached into the back of the jeep and pulled out a heavy box. Opening it, he drew out several bottles of green liquid. 'We'll be drinking this instead.'

He threw a couple to each of the lads. The contents seemed to glow brightly, like toxic waste in a cartoon.

'What *is* this?' Ryan wasn't sure that he wanted anything that colour inside him.

'*This* is our secret weapon.' Drew was proud of it.

'It's a mixture of everything you need to keep you going out here. It'll keep you hydrated, keep your body sugars up, and it'll also act as a gradual painkiller. It doubles your energy and stamina.'

Ryan looked again at the bottle. He guessed it made sense. Drew had been working on a special energy drink and his team planned to travel fast and light to the destination. No stopping and no sleeping; just walking through the night.

'Drink some,' ordered Sarrell, flipping the lid off his bottle. 'How much would you say, Drew?'

'A third of a bottle should get us going for now.' Drew knocked it back.

Ryan followed suit, warily lifting the bottle to his lips and taking a sip. It filled his mouth with a sour taste, a mixture of potent medicine and cat pee. He spat it out.

'Aw man, I can't drink that!' he gasped, wiping his eyes. 'That's grim!'

'Drink it, Jacobs. That's an order.' Sarrell gave him a fierce look.

Ryan, realising he was serious, lifted the bottle back up and forced himself to swallow.

It didn't get any better.

'I admit the taste isn't great,' said Drew, 'but otherwise it's pretty good for you.'

'Five minutes, cadets.' The soldier shouted over to them from the jeep. 'I suggest you get yourselves ready to start.'

Ryan tied his laces and then picked up the rucksack. He was relieved to discover it was much

112

lighter. However much he hated his team, he had to admit the plan they'd come up with was genius. They could win this thing, and he looked forward to seeing the look on Kev's face if they did.

The soldier looked at his watch.

'Ok cadets,' he said. 'You can begin. Good luck!'

***

Ryan's newfound optimism lasted a couple of hours. It was around the third steep hill he knew he was in trouble.

However hard he pushed himself, he couldn't keep up. His body was soaked with sweat, the straps of his rucksack rubbed against his shoulders, and he desperately needed a rest. He wiped his forehead with the back of his arm.

Drew was up front with Sarrell, almost dancing with energy. Stone marched along behind them. But Ryan trudged at the back, the distance between him and them growing wider with each step.

They were in an open grassy field. Cows stood at the other end, minding their own business. The light was fading, and Ryan would have been cold if he hadn't been moving so quickly. Now he could see why he didn't need his jacket.

As Sarrell reached the fence at the top of the hill, he turned to see Ryan trailing halfway across the field. 'JACOBS!' he yelled. 'GET HERE! NOW!'

Ryan picked up his pace as best he could, but his legs resisted, two hours of walking having already taken their toll.

'RUN!' ordered Sarrell.

Ryan broke into a reluctant jog, forcing himself up the hill. By the time he reached the others, he was out of breath.

Drew shook his head, a thin smile stretched across his rat-like face. 'Tut tut, Jacobs,' he mocked. 'Not good enough.'

'Any reason you're dragging your feet?' demanded Sarrell, grabbing hold of Ryan's vest and pulling him close so their faces almost touched.

'I—I'm tired,' admitted Ryan.

'You're tired?'

Without warning, Sarrell twisted his body and pushed Ryan face-down onto the grass. A fresh cow-pat lay inches away, and Sarrell forced Ryan's face towards it. Flies darted around.

'I'm sick of your excuses, Jacobs. Perhaps you need something to eat?' threatened Sarrell, his hand gripping the back of Ryan's hair and moving his head closer to the turd.

'No, please...' begged Ryan, trying to resist.

It was pointless. Sarrell pushed his head down hard and fast, rubbing it into the muck. The smell of moist animal dung filled Ryan's nostrils, making him gag until Sarrell finally let go.

Drew and Stone laughed as Ryan rolled on to his side, unsure if he was allowed to get up. He wiped the worst of the muck off his face with his bare arm, and ran his fingers through his hair, only making more of a mess.

'Nice look, Jacobs,' mocked Drew, shaking his head.

Meanwhile, Sarrell took out his bottle and had a swig of the green fluid.

'Take a drink, lads,' he said, 'and Drew, find a long stick.'

Drew looked at their leader curiously, but did as he was told, hunting at the edge of the field. He came back with a menacing looking weapon.

'That's perfect,' nodded Sarrell. 'You're going to need that, Drew, because I'm holding you responsible for ensuring that Jacobs keeps up with us.'

Drew glanced at the stick and then at Ryan. 'My pleasure,' he said, walking towards him. 'This is gonna be a lot of fun.'

Somehow, Ryan didn't feel the same way.

16. RIVER

THWACK!

Ryan yelped like a kicked puppy as Drew caught him across the back of the legs.

Darkness had fallen, and he'd been hit every time he slowed down. Ryan tried to go as fast as he could, but it wasn't fast enough for his team.

'Seriously, could you lay off?' He tried to sound reasonable, but it came out a lot more angry than he intended.

Drew laughed. 'Sure. If you go faster!' He raised the stick again, and Ryan dashed forwards a few steps, panting.

'Ok, ok,' he pleaded with Drew. 'I'll try. But why are we in such a hurry? I mean, we're sure to win aren't we? If we go through the night?'

'Other teams may do the same,' Stone replied.

'In fact,' added Sarrell, 'we're pretty sure one of the other teams *will* do that. Drew says someone else spent a long time in the chemistry lab this week.'

'Who?' asked Ryan, surprised that the team were talking to him for a change.

'Kirsty Riggs.'

The girl on Kev's team. Typical. That meant Kev

was still in with a chance of beating Ryan and winning the bet.

The lads were following a trail through the dark woods, their torches offering little more than a few metres visibility. Stone was leading the way, holding the map and compass and barely hesitating at each fork in the path. He had exceptional navigation skills, and they'd only had to stop once to double-check they hadn't taken a wrong turn. Ryan was behind him and he had to stay pretty close if he didn't want another caning from Drew, who was right on his heels. At the back was Sarrell.

They had to slow down a little as they descended a steep slope. Ryan traversed it on all fours, sliding most of the way on his backside. As the ground levelled out, he could see something glittering through the trees ahead.

The river.

'Time for a swim,' said Stone, dumping his rucksack on the bank and stripping off his clothes.

Ryan followed suit, glancing uneasily at the black water. It didn't look too deep, but he knew it would be freezing, just like the lake at Devonmoor.

Stone was naked within minutes and stuffed his clothes and boots in the top of his rucksack. He lifted the bag up high and made his way across. At one point the water reached Stone's chest. The lad let out a war whoop. 'Guys, this is *cold!*'

Ryan was standing on the bank in his underwear, hesitant to remove his last barrier of dignity with Drew and Sarrell so close, but it would be stupid not to take them off as they'd only get soaked.

'Feeling shy, Jacobs?' teased Drew, poking him with the stick.

'No,' lied Ryan, pulling down his boxers and turning away as he stuffed them and his other clothes into the bag before stepping into the water.

His legs felt as if they had been plunged into a bucket of ice and his teeth started chattering as he stumbled forwards. By now Stone had reached the opposite bank.

Just a couple of minutes, Ryan, he told himself. *You can do this.*

The water was halfway up his chest and Ryan thought about plunging his head under to wash off the cow muck, but he couldn't bring himself to do it—it was too cold to get his hair wet. Besides, he might drop the bag. His arms already ached from the effort of holding it up.

He forced his way forward, resisting the slow but powerful pull of the current, before emerging on the opposite bank of the river, dripping wet and shivering. He used his jacket as a towel before hurriedly pulling on his clothes.

By now Drew had also reached the shore.

'See what I mean, Drew,' laughed Stone, seeing the younger boy shivering. 'It's freezing!'

Drew didn't respond as he stepped out the water. Stone consulted the map and compass again, checking and double-checking their route. Ryan started tugging on his stupidly long socks, something he always hated. It was even worse this time because there were two pairs to deal with.

Sarrell reached the bank, unaffected by the temperature. 'I dunno what you boys are moaning about,' he bragged. 'You need to grow some balls.'

Stone laughed. Drew, however, stayed silent. He was half-dressed and sat down on the sharp stones with his head in his hands.

'Hey Drew,' ordered Sarrell, 'get a move on. We need to carry on walking.'

Ryan glanced up, pleased to see the ferret of a boy getting moaned at for a change.

Drew just sat there, rocking a little.

Sarrell, not happy at being ignored, headed over and grabbed him by the hair. 'I said, get dressed!'

And then it happened. Drew snapped. He screamed and brought his hand up from nowhere, plunging something into Sarrell's stomach. The older cadet stumbled backwards, shocked, his eyes wide as he looked down to see a sharp stick protruding from his flesh, blood streaming from the wound. Drew lunged forward and knocked him to the floor, punching him hard.

Ryan froze. Drew had gone crazy. He had the Fury.

Stone was quick off the mark. He picked up a large stick and circled towards Drew, his movements cold and calculated. 'I suggest you back off, Drew,' he warned, as they locked eyes. 'You're not thinking straight and I don't want to do this.'

Drew didn't seem to care. He let out a manic yell and launched himself at Stone. The stick made contact but Drew didn't even seem to feel it. He dragged the older cadet to the floor. They rolled around and there were sickening thuds as kicks and punches from both lads met their targets.

Ryan panicked. He'd been in a lot of trouble before, but he'd never been so afraid. If Stone lost the fight, then he'd be next, and he didn't stand a chance against the wild boy. A plan formed in his mind: He needed to let off the emergency flare. Sarrell and Stone's lives depended on it. So did his.

He reached inside his rucksack, grasping for the metal tube. To his relief he could feel the cold steel under his fingers. As he pulled it out, he glanced up and his blood ran cold.

Drew was a few metres away, standing over the unconscious body of Stone, his fists clenched and drool dripping from his half-open mouth. As Ryan watched, Drew turned towards him, an evil glint in his eyes.

You're next.

The world stood still.

Everything happened in slow motion.

Drew started towards him, and in desperation Ryan fired the flare straight at the younger boy's chest. With a flash of bright red sparks and a strangled yell, Drew fell backwards as it scraped past him and hit the tree behind, a firework gone amok.

While the boy was distracted, Ryan turned and fled into the woods, but soon realised that with no boots and no torch he wouldn't get far. He couldn't see as he stumbled along, his socks sliding and squelching in the wet mud. He needed to hide. Finding a small space behind a tree, Ryan hunched down.

There was no sign of Drew.

He waited.

Minutes passed, feeling like hours.

Still nothing.

And then—Ryan's heart pounding hard against his chest—he could hear someone creeping along, a short distance away. He froze, but it was no good: the boy could see him cowering against the tree.

Drew came towards him, his movement wild and erratic. It was hard to see but something wasn't right with Drew's face: part of it was burnt from the flare.

'I'm going to kill you...' he hissed as he came closer.

Ryan tried to run, but he'd only taken two steps before he slipped and his body slammed down in the mud. And now he was being dragged into the clearing by his ankle. He tried to pull away, but it made no difference.

Drew held his prey upside down, and started kicking Ryan hard in the face.

'No!' yelled Ryan, trying to shield his head with his arms. 'Don't do it, Drew! You've got the Fury! Fight it!'

But Drew kept kicking.

Ryan tried to squirm out of the way as the boot smashed into his cheek. That just made his stomach the next target. A few more blows and Drew let go, leaving Ryan sprawled in the dirt.

The mad boy picked up a large branch, lifting it

high like a club.

This is it, thought Ryan. *This is where it ends.*

He closed his eyes and waited for the inevitable pain and darkness. But instead, he felt the soft weight of Drew collapse onto him, his body lifeless and dull.

Ryan turned his head, confused. Soldiers were running towards them, one of them holding a tranquilliser gun.

'Are you alright, son?'

'I think so,' groaned Ryan. 'But the others...'

'Don't worry about them. They're being looked after.'

Lifting Drew's body off him, the soldier helped Ryan to stand up and half-carried him to a helicopter in a nearby clearing. It all felt like it was happening somewhere else, somewhere far away.

Ryan wondered if Sarrell and Stone were going to be ok.

And then he wondered why he cared.

17. BLAME

His ribs hurt.

Ryan moaned and rolled on to his side, clutching them with his arm. Gradually, he opened his eyes. One of them was swollen and would only open halfway.

He was in his bed at the academy.

Kev sat on the bunk above, looking down at him. 'So you're alive?'

'Just about,' croaked Ryan. He made to sit up but then thought better of it and lay back down on his side. 'Shouldn't I be in the medical room?'

Kev jumped down. 'Apparently, they're just cuts and bruises. No serious injuries according to Dr Fleur.'

Ryan touched his face, gingerly. 'No serious injuries? I feel like I've been run over.'

'Yeah, well you don't look that great either,' grinned Kev.

'Thanks.'

A pause. Then Ryan asked: 'Did anyone else get it? The Fury, I mean?'

'No, just Drew.' Kev raised his eyebrows. 'And you know what that means?'

'What?' asked Ryan.

'You, my friend, have a lot of laundry to do.' The older lad pointed to the corner of the room, where there was a large pile of muddy uniforms.

'Seriously?' Ryan's voice was higher pitched than he wanted it to be. 'Even though I'm injured? And we would have won if it wasn't for the Fury?'

'Suck it up, Jacobs,' Kev laughed. 'No excuses, no whining, remember? You agreed to the deal, now live with it.'

Ryan sat up, ignoring the pain. 'So how did your team do?'

'We won.' Kev was in a cocky mood and kicked Ryan's leg playfully with his socked foot. 'Ask me how.'

Ryan sighed. 'How?'

'We built a mini hot-air balloon! It was genius! Mark and Lee worked out that the wind would be in our favour so we floated several metres above ground and let it carry us and our bags to the finish line.'

'You're not serious?' Ryan couldn't believe it. When he'd suggested an aircraft, his team thought he was nuts.

'Completely.' Kev sat on the lower bunk opposite Ryan. 'Lee and Mark worked out all the mechanics back at the planning stage. I didn't know they had it in them. But it was something to behold, that's for sure. It's a shame Lee didn't get to see it in action.'

'How is Lee?'

'He's doing well. Should be back with us tonight. Anyway, you need to get up and showered. It's almost dinner-time.'

***

To Ryan's relief, the canteen was back to normal, and he could sit with his usual group of friends. Sparks, Ranjit, Kev, Jael and Ayana huddled in close as he recounted what had happened beside the river.

'Drew stabbed Sarrell?' Ayana shook her head. 'And I thought Lee was in trouble for hitting the colonel. I think Drew might have it worse. Sarrell is gonna destroy him.'

Ryan could see her point. 'Yeah, when he gets out of the medical room he is not going to be a happy cadet.'

'Mark, Lee, and now Drew...' puzzled Sparks, chewing on a tough piece of meat. 'Why them? Why no-one else?'

'It's random,' suggested Ranjit, 'like the flu. Some people are more vulnerable than others.'

'Maybe.' Sparks didn't seem convinced.

'It's happening to different people every couple of days,' pointed out Kev. 'The question is whether we're all going to get it.'

That shut everyone up as they thought of the implications of living at a school where people kept going crazy for no reason.

What if there was no end to it? No cure? What if a cadet woke up with the Fury in the middle of the night and attacked their roommates? What if someone got killed? No-one was going to sleep easy tonight.

As the mealtime ended, the colonel stood up and banged on the table for attention. The room fell silent.

'Cadets,' he boomed. 'You are no doubt aware that we have had another case of outrageous behaviour during the hike. One more cadet seems to have taken leave of his senses.' This wasn't news to anyone. 'This behaviour is unacceptable, and it needs to cease. The staff and I know that something unusual is going on, which is why we have chosen not to expel any cadets, *yet*. However, we still intend to make an example of them to discourage anyone else from doing the same.'

The colonel beckoned to the doorway and Lee and Mark shuffled forward like condemned men.

'Cadet Young and Cadet Collins,' said the colonel, addressing the boys. 'You are both guilty of violent and disorderly behaviour on a scale never seen before at this academy. As a punishment for your behaviour, you will clean up the dining hall and kitchen every evening by yourselves until I feel your debt has been paid.'

Ryan could see the resignation in the boys' faces. Cleaning up after a hundred cadets had eaten their dinner was a long job—it took hours. Doing it every night was a horrible prospect. Mark looked like he was going to be sick.

The colonel turned back to the rest of the cadets. 'If any of you wish to join them, then feel free to have one of these fits, or whatever they are. I should also warn you that we have armed all the prefects with tranquilliser guns for the time being, in case there are any more *episodes*.'

Ryan glanced over at Sarah on the next table and noticed that she was gripping a lethal-looking device.

'And,' added the colonel, nastily, 'they have been told to shoot first and ask questions later. If you show the slightest sign of anger or unusual behaviour, then you'll be shot. Do I hear any objections?'

No-one looked too happy about the idea of trigger-happy prefects running around the school but the students knew better than to speak up when the colonel was on one of his rants. Instead, there was a slight fidgeting and wary, fearful glances.

'No? Good. Dismissed.'

18. PATTERNS

Despite everyone being on edge, the next few days passed without incident.

Lessons returned to their normal pattern and the rhythm of academy life was restored. It would have been easy for everyone to forget about the Fury, had it not been for the constant vigilance of the prefects with their guns. Less than a week had gone by but people had already got bored and turned their attention to other things.

But it wasn't just boredom. It was as if everyone *wanted* to forget it—they wanted the issue to go away; to disappear with no explanation or answers. They wanted to live without fear.

That never worked for Ryan.

Meanwhile, now he was back out of the medical room, Sarrell had been appointed as a prefect as a reward for his bravery in rescuing Mr Cho from the wild monkey. The sight of Sarrell armed with a tranquilliser gun and a black beret sent a shiver down Ryan's spine.

Right now, Ryan was sitting in the computer lab, but was frustrated by Mr Davids' obsession with his new antivirus programme. The teacher kept hassling him about the problem and Ryan was losing interest.

'Sir, I really think it can't be done.'

'But it can, my boy! It must be possible! Difficult, yes, but possible.' Mr Davids strolled up and down the room muttering numbers to himself. Ryan slouched on an office chair with his feet on a nearby desk, aware that this was the only place in the academy he could do that with a teacher nearby.

'Not all transformations are reversible,' explained Ryan. 'You know that.'

Mr Davids turned and looked at him, as if noticing him for the first time. 'But it's all patterns! There are always patterns, always! To solve the problem all you need to do is find the pattern. Why has this particular number been changed in this way? Why this string of code and not that one? Patterns, you see?'

'Yes, sir.' He allowed his mind to wander a little, thinking back to the events of the previous week. Something was bugging him and he couldn't quite figure out what it was.

To solve the problem all you need to do is find the pattern...

Mark. Lee. Drew. Not much in common there. They lived in three different dormitories. Not all of them were around when the monkey went crazy. They were on different teams for the hike—well, Drew was anyway. Each had different specialisms. They were different ages.

'Drink?' Mr Davids jolted Ryan out of his thought process.

'Err, yeah, sure.' Ryan smiled as the teacher threw

him a can of Coke.

'I always find sugar helps me think. A bit of extra energy can't hurt...' The teacher cracked open his own can while staring at the code he had written on the whiteboard.

Memories surfaced in Ryan's mind as he thought about the three lads who had suffered from the Fury.

Sugar helps me think... a bit of extra energy can't hurt...

All three of them got a lot smarter before they went crazy. Mark had beaten Jael at chess. Lee had helped design a working hot-air balloon. Ryan didn't know if that had happened to Drew as well, but it wasn't impossible. They all had loads of energy. Lee had been doing press-ups in the middle of the night and Drew had been unstoppable on the hike.

A pattern. Increased mental capacity and tremendous amounts of physical activity. Then the Fury.

So, what was the cause? Something that boosted your brain-power, or that made you energetic?

It all clicked into place and Ryan jumped up. 'Sorry sir, I have to go.'

***

The science labs were empty. Ryan checked the store cupboard and the area with the caged animals, desperate to find Mr Cho. Kirsty walked in, almost colliding with him, her hands full of books and papers.

'Oh, sorry.' Ryan hadn't chatted to Kirsty before,

but she'd probably know where Mr Cho was. She spent as much time in the science labs as he did on the computers. 'Congratulations on winning the hike. Kev said you were awesome on the team.'

'Thanks.' Kirsty smiled, shyly.

'Any idea where I can find Mr Cho?'

'He's away today,' replied the younger girl. 'He's at a conference. He'll be back tomorrow.'

Ryan swore and looked away.

'Maybe I can help?' Kirsty put her books down on a nearby table. 'I know quite a bit about science.'

That was an understatement. Kirsty was a scientific genius if the rumours at the academy were true. Ryan decided to trust her. 'Ok, I think I know what's causing the Fury.' Kirsty glanced around uneasily, but Ryan pressed on. 'Listen. Drew developed this drink for the hike. It was bright green. Meant to make you super-energetic so we could walk through the night. I figure he'd drunk way more of it than the rest of us and it sent him mad.'

'Sounds possible,' admitted Kirsty. 'He was working on that all last week. But what about Mark and Lee?'

'I'm not sure, but maybe he got them to drink it— to test it. And maybe he tested it on that monkey?'

'It's a decent theory.' Kirsty spent a few moments thinking it through. 'Do we have any of the drink? I could analyse it and see if you're right.'

'Afraid not. Not unless he has any stashed away up here?'

Kirsty looked over to the far corner. 'He may have

some in his locker?'

Ryan followed her to the metal cabinet. A small padlock held it shut. 'Got anything heavy?'

'Probably. There must be something around here.' Kirsty hunted in some drawers. After a while, she handed him a large rock. 'I think this was being used by some of the geology specialists.'

Ryan examined it. 'It's perfect.' He slammed the rock down hard on the padlock. It took several attempts to smash it off, but eventually he succeeded.

'Won't we get in trouble for this?' asked Kirsty, looking worried.

'Maybe,' admitted Ryan. Then, seeing the concern on her face he added: 'If anyone asks, blame me.'

Drew wasn't the tidiest person in the world and the locker was stuffed full of screwed up paper, a dirty lab coat, gloves and other items. But there amongst it all were a couple of bottles of the bright green fluid.

'Win!' exclaimed Ryan and handed one to Kirsty.

'Ok, I'll run some tests.'

'Great. Just don't let Drew know what you're up to.'

Kirsty looked offended. 'Of course. I'm not stupid.'

'Sorry.' Ryan felt awkward. 'I meant because he's violent. I don't want to put you in any danger.'

'Ok. Sure. I'll be careful.'

There was a pause—neither of them knew what to say for a moment. Ryan's thoughts returned to the task.

'How long will it take?' he asked.

'A couple of days. It's a slow process.'

That wasn't what he wanted to hear, but there

wasn't a lot he could do. 'Fine. Let me know if you find anything. And Kirsty... thanks. I really appreciate it.'

She looked up at him with an odd smile before turning and walking over to the desk.

Ryan couldn't be sure, but he sensed she was thinking about something other than the Fury.

He thought she might be thinking about him.

19. REMEDIAL

Saturday.

Ryan dreaded the Devonmoor assault course at the best of times. It was on this course that he'd had some kind of fit as he crawled through a cramped tunnel. It's never good to wet yourself in front of the kids at your school, and he still got teased about it.

He stood at the edge of the clearing by the first obstacle, alongside Drew, Stone and Sarrell, all wearing the blue-and-yellow academy sports kit. The sky was grey: it was probably going to rain, just to make the morning even more miserable.

The colonel glared at them. 'Well, cadets,' he began, with relish. 'As your team failed to finish the hike, it is time for your remedial teamwork classes to begin. Working together can be such a joy and I think it's important that you grow to appreciate that.' He paused, looking them up and down. 'You are going to complete the assault course together. And you're going to do it in a respectable time. Sergeant Wright?'

The sergeant, standing nearby, stepped forward and approached the lads. To Ryan's horror he pulled a few pairs of handcuffs from his pockets and proceeded to cuff the boys to each other. Ryan's wrist was chained to Drew on one side and Sarrell on the other.

'You need to complete the course in under nineteen minutes.'

Ryan felt Drew and Sarrell tense; they both knew that what the colonel was asking was far from realistic. They wanted to object, but there was no point. The colonel would only make it worse.

'Is there a problem?' The colonel raised his eyebrows.

'No, sir,' Sarrell replied. 'But is it possible, with us handcuffed together like this?'

'I guess we'll find out, won't we?' asked the colonel, with a wicked smile. 'If we don't manage it in the next few hours, we can try again next week. And then the week after.'

Ryan's heart sank. It could take months.

'And before you get any ideas,' said the colonel, looking directly at Ryan, 'I've had enough of you skiving out of doing the parts you don't like. Today, you will do the entire course, tunnels included. Do you understand?'

'Yes, sir,' said Ryan. His legs started shaking.

'You can start on Sergeant Wright's whistle.'

It only took a few minutes to realise how hard it was going to be.

Crossing the ditch by walking over a large log was tricky when you couldn't move your arms freely. If any of them fell, then the rest of the team would follow. That made Ryan nervous as he looked down at the filthy knee-deep muck below. Sarrell and the others wouldn't thank him if he slipped and dragged them into that.

The next obstacle was a five-foot wall; that was much more of a challenge. It took them several failed attempts to get across. The handcuffs prevented any kind of simple movement, and there was a lot of cursing as various limbs scraped over the top of the logs. Ryan was sure it wasn't safe: it was a miracle no-one broke their arm. By the time they'd finished, he guessed that they'd taken ten minutes trying to do that obstacle alone. There was no way they were going to finish the entire course in under nineteen.

'Move it!' ordered Sarrell. He yanked the others forward, the cuffs digging into Ryan's wrists.

They headed back to the ditch where a set of tyres hung from ropes. They had to step from one to the other, using them as footholds as they crossed. Sarrell and Ryan got started, but a couple of tyres in, Drew slipped and fell. That meant the whole team were pulled backwards, off the tyres and into the mud. Ryan felt the stagnant filth soak through the back of his rugby shirt, and by the time he'd stood up, most of his body was dripping with muck. The boys trudged back to dry ground.

'You idiot!' Sarrell shouted at Drew, using his free hand to smack the younger lad's head.

They heard a mocking laugh and looked up to see the colonel standing over them, next to Sergeant Wright. 'You don't know how funny this is to watch,' he observed, as they crawled up the bank, side by side. 'And we've only been going for thirteen minutes!

I think we're in for an entertaining few hours.'

None of the lads responded; there was nothing to say. Sarrell pulled them back to the tyre swings. They started across again, this time with Drew managing to keep his foothold.

Now for the obstacle Ryan was dreading: the tunnel.

'Jacobs, you better not freak out in here else there's gonna be hell to pay,' growled Sarrell, pulling him forwards.

Ryan was too scared to respond. He closed his eyes and kept moving, forcing one knee in front of another, being pulled by Sarrell in front and pushed by Drew from behind. His face was right next to Sarrell's wet and muddy trainers as they inched through the tunnel.

It was dark, and cramped, and he started to panic. *Don't think about it, Ryan.*

He tried to remember the mental exercises that Dr Torren had taught him to cope with these situations: *You're in a safe, warm place and you feel relaxed.*

It was hard to imagine that as his arms and legs scraped the edges of the tunnel and all he could smell was stagnant ditch water. But Sarrell pulled him through at such a speed that he didn't have time to dwell on it. He emerged at the other end of the tunnel shaking but conscious.

'Looks like Jacobs made it through the tunnel without wetting himself,' commented Sergeant Wright. 'See what a little teamwork can do?'

Ryan face burned, but he kept his mouth shut as

Sarrell pulled them on.

***

The first time they finished the assault course it took them forty-three minutes, over double the time they were allowed. The second time was much faster at twenty-nine, but still much too slow to meet their target. By then, they were exhausted, bruised and in no shape to carry on.

'One more attempt,' ordered Sergeant Wright. 'And then we'll call it a day. You can return here next week for another go. I think you're going to know this course pretty well in a couple of months!'

Their last attempt was pretty feeble. Sarrell took them tumbling into the ditch at one point, losing his balance on the log. By now, they were all shivering and covered in mud.

'Well, that's it.' The sergeant tapped his watch as they crossed the finish line. 'Thirty-three minutes. Another fail.'

He stepped forward and undid the handcuffs. Ryan rubbed his sore wrists.

'Go and get changed lads, and be back here at the same time next week.'

***

The changing room was not a cheerful place.

'We're going to do it. We have to. I'm not coming out here every weekend.' Sarrell was fuming as he stripped off his filthy sports kit.

'We stand a much better chance now that we've worked out how to deal with the obstacles,' observed Stone. 'It'll be much easier next time.'

'I still don't think it will be enough.' Sarrell slumped down on the bench.

'Can't you speak to the colonel?' asked Ryan.

'Suck up to him, you mean?' spat Sarrell.

'I just thought he might listen to you.'

'You think that because I'm the colonel's favourite student, I can persuade him to go easy on us.' Sarrell said it with disgust.

'It's just an idea.' Ryan couldn't see how it would hurt.

'I should explain something to you, Jacobs. Colonel Keller and I have an understanding.' Sarrell pulled off his wet, muddy socks and flung them at Ryan. 'When I arrived at this academy I asked the colonel to toughen me up. I wanted to be treated worse than any other cadets. I told him to have higher expectations of me, to give me harsher punishments.'

'Seriously?' That sounded like a crazy idea to Ryan.

'I also told him that if I ever tried to back out of our deal or showed any weakness, he should get harsher still. When he realised I was serious, he agreed. My first few years at this academy were hard. He kept his side of the deal, and I kept mine. Now, he respects me, but the deal still stands.'

Ryan was horrified. 'So, if you ask him to go easy on us...'

'He'll make it worse.' Sarrell rubbed his face with his hands. 'We won't be getting out of doing the assault course any time soon.'

'Wait a minute,' piped up Drew. 'We could use the drink I made, the one that makes you super-active. That'll give us an edge.'

Ryan shuddered. The idea of being cuffed to guys who could get the Fury made him feel sick. What if Sarrell went crazy while they were chained together? What if it happened when they were in the tunnel?

'That might work.' Sarrell looked thoughtful.

'I don't think we should cheat,' said Ryan. 'The colonel will go nuts if he finds out.'

Sarrell grabbed Ryan by the neck and pushed him against the tiled wall. 'Are you calling me a cheater?'

'No,' gasped Ryan. 'I just thought the colonel might view it that way.'

'There are no rules against using Drew's drink. And, just so you know, I *never* cheat.'

'O-Ok,' said Ryan, and Sarrell dropped him to the floor.

'Bring the drink with you next week, Drew.' Sarrell's eyes narrowed. 'And if any of you let me down, then there will be blood. Lots of blood.'

20. STUPID

As soon as Ryan left the changing rooms, he ran up the stairs to the science labs. He was desperate to find Kirsty. He needed to know for sure whether Drew's invention was causing the Fury before his next session on the assault course.

To his frustration, the labs were empty and Kirsty was nowhere to be seen.

Come on, Ryan. Think!

He was convinced that the drink was dangerous, and he had to stop his team from using it.

Ryan headed over to Drew's locker in the corner and pulled it open. He grabbed the remaining couple of bottles of bright green fluid, hoping that these were the last ones. He had to get rid of them fast, before Drew came to fetch them.

'Cadet Jacobs!' The stern voice shocked Ryan, and he dropped the bottles on the floor. Fortunately, they were plastic, so they didn't smash. Ryan turned to see Mr Cho approaching. The teacher had a bandage over one side of his face. 'Does that belong to you, Jacobs?'

'No, sir.' Ryan felt his face turning bright red. He couldn't have looked more guilty if he tried.

'Well, boy, I'm assuming you have a good reason for breaking into another cadet's locker?'

Ryan had little choice now but to tell the truth. 'I think this is what's causing the Fury, sir. Drew's invention is putting everyone at risk.'

'I see.' Mr Cho sat down on a stool. 'Ryan, do I look stupid to you?'

The standard teacher script. Ryan played along. He was curious where this was going.

'No, sir.'

'And the other teachers at this academy. Do you think they're stupid?' It was a pointless question. Devonmoor employed the best teachers in the country—the Project relied on it.

'No sir. Not at all.'

'So,' said Mr Cho, 'when someone on the hike gets the Fury, as you refer to it, and we find his rucksack loaded with bright green liquid, don't you think we might be suspicious that there could be a link between the two?'

Ryan stayed silent.

'We tested it, Jacobs. We tested all of it: every bottle. It's not that impressive. Just a stimulant drink, not dissimilar to one you could buy in a supermarket. There's no way it's causing the Fury. If I was to grade Drew's invention, I would give it an E.'

Ryan looked at the floor, feeling dumb. Of course the teachers would have checked the drink. If they thought the students were taking drugs then that's the first thing they'd have done. 'Sorry, sir, I just thought...' Ryan trailed off, unsure what else to say.

'You just thought you were being cleverer than anyone else.'

'I guess so.'

'Put the bottles back, Jacobs. And if you have any other wild theories, then at least think of sharing them with me before you take action.'

'Yes, sir.' Ryan opened Drew's locker and replaced the drink. Mr Cho wandered over to his desk and busied himself with some paperwork. The conversation was over. Ryan was relieved that Mr Cho wasn't going to punish him; he left the science labs before the teacher changed his mind.

His head was reeling: his theory was wrong. It hadn't been Drew's drink at all.

And yet something wasn't quite right.

Something was nagging at the back of his mind.

If only he could figure out what it was.

***

The afternoon was pretty relaxed by Devonmoor standards, but Ryan found himself restless and unable to settle. He wandered from the school library to the common room, and then back to his dorm, not sure what to do. He needed to clear his head, but nothing was working.

Normally, he'd have gone to the computer lab. Right now, though, he was avoiding Mr Davids, not wanting to spend hours on a pointless problem. It was giving him a headache.

That meant there were two problems to solve, two

riddles without an answer. And his head wouldn't let them go. What was causing the Fury? And was there any solution to the antivirus code? He lay on his bed for a while, tossing and turning as he thought it through.

By dinner-time he was in a foul mood, resigned to another long week at Devonmoor followed by a couple of painful hours on the assault course. Meanwhile, the Fury cast its shadow over the school like a black cloud, everyone waiting for the next outburst. To top it off, he had loads of laundry, especially now he had yet another mud-soaked sports kit to get clean.

'You alright, Ryan?' asked Sparks, shovelling his mouth full of mashed potato.

'Not really.' Ryan wasn't sure where to start.

Ranjit leaned over, a concerned look in his eyes. 'Is it true you had to do the assault course handcuffed to the rest of your team?'

Ryan nodded and grimaced. 'We have to go back next Saturday and try again. And then the weekend after that. And so on. For months, probably.'

The others fell silent for a moment, like they were remembering a fallen comrade. Sparks finished the mouthful of potato. 'At least you get to see Sarrell and Drew go through it as well!'

'Yeah. That's true.' Ryan smiled a little. 'I've never seen Sarrell so annoyed with the colonel.'

'Their first lovers' tiff!' jested Sparks, and everyone laughed.

'Anyway,' announced Kev. 'We're flying our hot-air

balloon in the school grounds tomorrow if anyone wants to see it in action? We may give you a ride if you're lucky.'

This gained an excited response from the others, and Ryan figured there would be worse ways to spend a Sunday afternoon.

'How about you, Ryan? You in?' asked Kev. 'Or are you too busy doing laundry?'

The other lads laughed while Ryan playfully stuck up two fingers before standing up and heading out of the canteen. He'd barely stepped into the corridor before someone grabbed his arm and pulled him to one side. It was Kirsty, and she looked frantic.

'Kirsty, I—'

'Shh.' The girl put her hand up to his mouth. 'Don't say anything. We need to talk. I've found something in Drew's drink. You were right, Ryan! That's what's causing the Fury.'

'But—' Ryan started, but she wasn't listening.

'Meet me in the science labs in half an hour. Don't tell anyone you're coming.' She looked into his eyes, a look of concern and fear. 'Ryan, you have to trust me. This is serious. Promise me you'll come?'

'Ok, I'll come.' Ryan could hardly say no to her when she was so upset.

'Thank you.'

Kirsty darted away, leaving Ryan standing shocked and confused against the wall. Why would Mr Cho say the drink was harmless and Kirsty say it was dangerous? Who was wrong here? Who was lying?

And why?

21. LIES

It was getting dark outside as Ryan returned to the science labs. He had a tense feeling in his stomach.

Kirsty was working alone. An impressive array of test tubes, flasks and beakers were set out in front of her, blue liquid bubbling away over a bunsen burner. It was like a scene from a science fiction movie.

Ryan walked in, leaving the door ajar. He didn't want to break her concentration. 'Hey.'

She looked up, relieved to see him. 'Ryan! I'm so glad you came!' She took off her goggles and stepped back from the experiment.

'What's up?' he asked.

'It's the drink!' exclaimed Kirsty. 'You were right. There are drugs in there which stimulate the brain. But the problem is they're too strong and they cause a violent reaction. I'm trying to sort out a cure right now.' She rubbed her nose. 'We have to work out what we're going to do.'

Ryan walked over and put a hand on her shoulder. 'Kirsty, you don't need to lie to me,' he said, gently. 'I know it was you all along.'

She looked up at him, her eyes wide. 'I don't know what you mean? How could it be me? What are you—

'Listen,' Ryan cut in. 'I know it's nothing to do with Drew's drink. It's something you've been working on, isn't it? And it went wrong? And now you're trying to cover your tracks.'

Tears filled Kirsty's eyes, and she slumped down on a lab stool. 'How—how—how did you...?'

'I worked it out. Drew said you were in the labs the week before the hike, but your team won using a hot-air balloon. So what were you doing all that week? And then there was the fact that two of your team members got the Fury. You put it in their drinks so that they'd have better ideas for the hike, didn't you?'

Kirsty started sobbing. 'I thought it was safe... I thought I'd solved the problem after the monkey went crazy... I didn't mean to hurt anyone...'

Ryan hesitated and then put his arm around her, feeling a little awkward. 'I know. I figured that. But I guess when Mark and Lee went wild you knew it wouldn't take long before people worked out you were behind it, being on the same team. That's when you slipped some to Drew, to throw them off the scent. It can't have been difficult, working here in the same lab.'

'I-I-I was trying to work on a solution, but I couldn't find one. It's all I could think of.'

'Well it worked,' said Ryan. 'No-one suspected you. But now you need to come clean. You have to own up.'

'I know, I know...' sniffed Kirsty, hugging Ryan tightly. 'But there's something I have to do first.'

'What's that?'

Ryan felt a sharp stabbing pain in his shoulder-blade as Kirsty sank a needle into his back. 'What the—'

'Sorry, Ryan.' Kirsty wiped her eyes and stood up, her expression cold. 'More is at stake here than you realise. I need to test my new solution. And you just volunteered.'

The tears had all been fake, a ploy to keep him close. Ryan's legs gave way as his body grew numb and Kirsty lowered him to the floor. He stared at the underside of a lab stool, unable to move or speak.

'That was a shot of tranquilliser,' explained Kirsty, standing over him. 'Nothing to worry about.'

She grabbed another syringe off the table, this one containing a red solution. She flicked it. 'This, however, is my latest creation. It's time to see whether I've got rid of the undesirable side effects, or whether I've made them worse.'

Ryan tried to speak but only let out a low moan.

He didn't feel a thing as she injected it into his arm.

His world turned black.

***

When Ryan came to, he felt light-headed and his body ached. He could smell animals nearby: the aroma of damp hay, dung and rotten food.

Kirsty had dragged him over to one of the empty animal cages and locked him in. Monkeys leapt around on either side, the wire mesh preventing them from reaching through to where Ryan was.

He pulled himself into a sitting position, putting his hand in something wet and slimy as he did so. He wiped it on his trousers in disgust. The cage was cramped, and the floor was covered in hay and animal droppings. It was dark outside.

Kirsty was standing nearby, and seeing Ryan move, she headed over. 'How is the subject?' she asked, holding up a clipboard.

'You're insane,' he muttered. 'Let me out!'

'I can't. You don't know what's at stake,' explained Kirsty. 'The brain-enhancer is a scientific breakthrough, but I have to stop the side effects.'

'And how are you gonna do that?' asked Ryan.

'I think I've already done it.' Kirsty gave off a hollow laugh that was far from reassuring. 'At least, let's hope so, for your sake.'

Ryan felt his stomach turn to ice. 'But doesn't it take days to work?'

'Not with the amount you've had.' Kirsty leaned towards the cage, her eyes glinting. 'You're about to become much more intelligent, Ryan. And then you'll either get the Fury or you won't. We'll know in a couple of hours, which is why you need to stay in there.'

'You can't do this!' Ryan kicked at the cage door in frustration, but it was solid. There was no chance of breaking out. He couldn't even stretch out in the cramped space. He started to sweat, feeling trapped. 'What makes you think you've solved the problem now?' he asked. 'What did you do different this time?'

Kirsty glanced back at him, a wry smile on her face. 'Let's just say that I had a bit of help.'

'From who?'

Kirsty ignored him.

Who would have helped her?

Ryan fidgeted in the hay, aware that he was sitting in something grim. He watched Kirsty. She was making frantic notes and mixing the contents of test tubes. He noticed her hands were shaking.

Suddenly, he understood. Just when he thought his situation couldn't get any worse. She started pacing up and down the lab, wandering over to check on him.

'Kirsty,' urged Ryan, 'you have to listen to me.'

'I don't have to do anything!' laughed Kirsty.

'Did you take the brain-enhancer yourself? To solve the problem?'

'Maybe.' Her face gave the game away. She was on it alright.

'And you used the old stuff? The stuff which gives you the Fury?'

'Yeah, so what?'

'If you go mad while I'm stuck in here then you'll kill me,' said Ryan. He tried to sound calm and reasonable, but it was hard in the circumstances. 'Let me out. Please.'

Kirsty thought for a moment. 'That stuff does make you clever, Ryan. You almost convinced me. The thing is, I'm not due to go crazy for at least a day, so you're safe.'

Ryan leaned forward as best he could in the cramped space. 'But you're already shaking. You're gonna flip at any second! You have to let me out!'

Kirsty looked at her hands, and then back up at him. She ran her fingers through her hair and started muttering under her breath. Then she threw back her head and laughed.

Ryan panicked. He'd seen these signs before. 'Calm down, Kirsty. It's ok. Don't get worked up.'

It was no use. She'd gone over the edge. She picked up a glass beaker and threw it at Ryan. It smashed on the bars, showering him with broken glass. He shielded his eyes with his arm as the shards came flying towards him.

'KIRSTY! STOP!'

But she didn't. She ran over to a shelf full of chemicals and grabbed a large jar full of yellow liquid, before advancing back towards Ryan's cage. Even from where he was sitting, Ryan could see that it had a frightening label.

'I'm going to burn you...' she hissed, caressing the jar, her eyes wild with rage.

Ryan's heart was in his mouth. He pressed his body against the bars but there was no way out.

The wild girl lifted her arm, preparing to shower Ryan with acid. There was nothing he could do, nowhere to go.

He was going to die.

Or be permanently scarred.

Either way it was *really* going to hurt.

22. ENEMY

It happened at the last possible moment, when Ryan had lost all hope. Kirsty crashed to the floor, losing consciousness, the jar smashing on the floor behind her, a horrible hissing noise erupting from the tiles as the contents spilled.

And there he was: James Sarrell.

Cocky as ever, the older cadet caught hold of the unconscious Kirsty and dragged her away from the danger zone. Ryan could see a tranquilliser dart sticking out her back.

Sarrell dumped the girl on the other side of the room and sauntered back to where Ryan sat trapped.

'Nice cage,' he sneered. 'It suits you.'

'I thought you weren't coming!' exclaimed Ryan, his fear turning to anger. 'I thought you were going to let me die!'

'I did consider it,' admitted Sarrell. 'But where's the fun in that? I wouldn't get to kick you around for the next few years. Besides, if anyone is going to pour acid over you then it's going to be me, Jacobs.'

Ryan tried to calm down. He should be thanking Sarrell. 'So you just watched all of that?' he asked, his voice strained. 'And you decided not to intervene any earlier? I mean, you figured you'd let her inject me and then put me in a cage.'

'Pretty much.' Sarrell pulled up a stool and sat down. 'It amused me. Besides, you weren't in any real danger.'

Ryan breathed deeply. 'Fine,' he said. 'Thanks for the rescue. So, are you gonna let me out or what?'

Sarrell smirked. 'You heard the girl, Ryan. You've got an advanced version of her new drug in you. You could go psycho at any moment. You're not going anywhere.'

'But can't you get the teachers? They could put me in a straight-jacket, or in the medical room?'

'Yes,' soothed Sarrell, 'wouldn't that be nice? But nowhere near as entertaining as watching you go crazy in a cage.'

'You're actually serious?' Ryan couldn't believe what he was hearing. He gripped the bars, his knuckles white. 'You know I'm claustrophobic! I can't stand it in here.'

'That's what's going to make this *so* entertaining.' Sarrell stood up and headed back towards the main science lab. 'I'll be back soon. Don't go anywhere.'

'Wait? Where are you going?'

Sarrell gave an evil grin. 'Well,' he said. 'First, I need to get Kirsty to the medical room. Then I'll be back to watch the show.' He picked up Kirsty, hauled her over his shoulder and headed out of the lab.

Alone in the cage, Ryan tried to think about anything other than his surroundings. His feeble attempts to pick the lock had failed, and he right now

Sarrell was his only hope for getting out before morning. No-one came to the science labs at night.

He was lucky to be alive. That didn't mean that he *felt* lucky, crammed into the cage with animals screeching around him.

His breathing was erratic. Sweat dripped down his back. Any moment, the memories would come flooding back. He had to think about something else. Anything else.

He longed to be back in the computer lab, away from the noise and the smell of the animals. But then he'd have to face Mr Davids and the virus problem. The one that couldn't be solved.

Or could it...

The more Ryan thought, the more he saw what Mr Davids meant. There would always be a pattern. He closed his eyes and visualised the numbers in his head. Things started falling into place, clearer than ever. The brain-enhancing drug began to work. He could solve this!

By the time Sarrell returned, Ryan was frantic: 'Sarrell! Thank God you're here. I need some paper! Give me paper and a pen! Right now!' He was afraid he'd forget the crucial piece of code as soon as the drug wore off.

Sarrell leaned against the opposite wall, his head cocked to one side. He smirked at Ryan through the bars. 'Want to do some homework, Jacobs?'

'Please, Sarrell. This is important. I'm begging you. I need to write something.'

Sarrell thought for a moment and then gave Ryan

a sly look. 'Ok, how about a deal? If I give you some paper and a pen then you agree not to go whining to any teachers about spending all night in this cage? And you let me take all the credit for working out what caused the Fury.'

'What!? No way! That's out of order.' Ryan grabbed the bars and tried to kneel upright but all he managed to do was bang his head before landing back on his backside.

Sarrell laughed. 'Fine. No paper and pen then.'

Ryan was desperate. 'Ok. Sure. Whatever. Anything. You get all the credit. No complaints.'

'You swear on your honour?' Sarrell was serious.

'I swear.'

'I'm trusting you on this, Jacobs,' nodded Sarrell. He wandered over to a desk and picked up an old exercise book and a pen. He threw them at Ryan, who scrabbled for them amongst the pile of monkey droppings before scribbling down some equations.

'You're one hell of a geek, you know that, Jacobs? I hope it's worth it. It's going to be a long night.'

Ryan didn't respond; his head was swimming in a world of numbers and digits, lost to his grim surroundings.

***

It was still dark when Ryan opened his eyes, but the emergency exit sign gave off just enough light for him to see.

The cage was cold and uncomfortable—every part

of his body ached. He was covered in bruises. He tried to stretch but the bars only allowed him to extend his legs so far. His head pounded; he groaned and looked around. There was no sign of Sarrell.

His academy uniform was ruined. It had been torn to pieces. Much worse was the smell: he'd gone nuts in here, ripping his own clothes and rolling around in the monkey dung. There was a strange taste in his mouth.

This was not good.

Thankfully, he could see the exercise book had been thrown out of the cage; he had a vague memory of doing that in his last sane moments before the Fury kicked in. He hoped he could make sense of what he wrote.

'Sarrell?' Ryan shouted, but there was no response.

He shifted his weight and tried to wipe the worst of the hay and dirt off himself, but it was pointless.

There was no way of knowing what time it was or how long Sarrell would leave him here. He cursed under his breath.

And then he did the only other thing he could do.

He waited.

***

Hours later, Ryan heard the door open. Sarrell strutted towards the cage. 'Have a good night's sleep, Jacobs?'

'You've had your fun. Let me out.'

'You remember our deal, right?' Sarrell's voice was hard.

'Sure. You get to be the hero.'

'Good.' Sarrell pulled a small device out of his pocket. 'And just in case you're tempted to change your mind, I recorded you having your little fit last night. Makes for entertaining viewing, watching you roll around in the filth. I particularly enjoyed the moment when you ate some of it.'

The colour drained from Ryan's face. 'You're not going to show that to anyone are you?' he asked with a weak voice.

'Not unless you break our deal. Or the mood takes me.'

Sarrell reached down and unlocked the cage. Ryan stumbled out.

'You'll be called to Lady Devonmoor's office this morning, so be sure to make me look good.'

'Whatever,' muttered Ryan. 'How long do I have until drill?'

Sarrell gave a wicked grin. 'About eleven minutes.'

Ryan swore, then turned and ran from the lab as fast as his legs would carry him.

***

The boys' dormitory was frantic with activity when Ryan crashed through the door.

'Ryan! What on earth...' started Kev.

'Miss me?' asked Ryan, stripping off his ruined uniform and grabbing clean clothes from the wardrobe.

'Sarrell said you were being kept in the medical room. He told us you had the Fury.'

'Well let's just say it's been a pretty grim night. I'll tell you the gory details later.' Ryan brushed his hair as best he could, trying to make himself presentable.

'Mate, what is that smell?' Lee screwed up his face in disgust.

'Don't ask,' replied Ryan. 'Trust me, you don't want to know.'

23. REWARD

Sarrell was already in Lady Devonmoor's office when Ryan arrived. He was sitting in a soft armchair, looking pleased with himself. The colonel, Dr Torren and Lady Devonmoor were sipping tea from fragile-looking china cups.

'Ah, Ryan, do come in,' smiled the headteacher. 'Take a seat, dear.'

Ryan slumped into one of the soft armchairs.

'Cadet Sarrell explained to us how he solved the mystery of the Fury,' explained the doctor, 'and how you helped him catch Kirsty.'

'Yeah, sure,' muttered Ryan. 'It was nothing.' He wasn't too sure what Sarrell had said, and what he hadn't told them. He needed to tread carefully.

Sarrell could see the difficulty and offered Ryan a little help. 'When I needed someone to go in as bait to test my theory, I knew Ryan would be up for it. He's brave like that. Headstrong.'

'More arrogant than headstrong I'd say,' muttered the colonel.

'So you two worked together on this?' Dr Torren looked puzzled. 'You were happy to work with Sarrell, Ryan? You trusted him?'

'Yeah, sure.' Ryan forced out the words. 'Really happy.'

Until he nearly let me get covered in acid, and then left me in a cage.

The truth was that he had needed Sarrell, and he *had* trusted him to a point. Once he'd worked out that Kirsty was behind the Fury, he guessed he might need backup when he confronted her. He needed someone with access to a tranquilliser gun and who wouldn't be afraid to use it.

Lady Devonmoor looked at the colonel and Dr Torren. 'You see,' she smiled. 'I told you that this teamwork week was a good idea. Who would have thought that these two cadets would work together on anything? If they can overcome their differences to solve a problem, then the Project can continue to be a success!'

Sarrell glanced at Ryan, a slight warning in his eyes.

'It was all Sarrell's doing,' interjected Ryan, keen to ensure he kept his end of the deal. 'He worked out that it was Kirsty, and how we could get her to confess. And he saved my life when she went crazy. I'd be dead if it wasn't for him.'

'You didn't mention that part, Sarrell?' inquired the colonel.

Sarrell relaxed a little. 'It was no big deal.'

'You're becoming quite the hero at Devonmoor.' Dr Torren kept a neutral expression, but Ryan could see that the teacher was suspicious. Lady Devonmoor and the colonel were too caught up in the moment to notice the doctor's tone.

'He is indeed!' clapped Lady Devonmoor. 'We shall have to reward him, don't you think, Colonel?'

'Definitely.'

'In fact, I can think of no-one more deserving of the Devonmoor Cross.'

The Devonmoor Cross was the academy's highest award, given to the bravest students. Only two previous cadets had ever achieved it in the school's history.

'We'll present it to him during drill next week,' agreed the colonel.

'Well,' said Dr Torren, cutting in. 'Perhaps we should also reward both Jacobs and Sarrell by relieving them of their remedial teamwork classes. After all, I think these cadets have proved beyond a doubt that they can work together.'

'I suppose so,' said the colonel, a little reluctant.

Ryan could have hugged Dr Torren for that suggestion. Something good had come out of this at least. But there was one thing he had to know. 'What about Kirsty?' he asked. 'What will happen to her?'

A knowing look passed between the teachers.

'Kirsty will be leaving the academy,' explained Lady Devonmoor, 'and she won't be coming back. She endangered the Project.'

'She'll be expelled? You're sending her home?'

'Not home, Jacobs. Somewhere else.' The colonel almost smiled as he said it: *Be afraid, Jacobs. You're next. I will get you kicked out of Devonmoor. And you won't be going home. You'll be going somewhere worse. Much worse.*

'Blackfell?' Ryan almost whispered the words. He remembered being threatened with the place when he'd first arrived at the academy.

No-one responded. An awkward silence descended on the room.

'Well,' said the doctor, 'the important thing is, at least no more students will go crazy from now on.'

'Things can return to normal,' agreed the colonel.

'Thanks to both of you,' smiled Lady Devonmoor. 'This is a good day for Devonmoor. Tea, anyone?'

***

As Ryan left the office, he turned to Sarrell. 'Ok?' he asked. 'Was that good enough for you?'

'It'll do,' nodded Sarrell.

'So we're good now?' prompted Ryan. 'You'll leave me alone.'

Without warning, Sarrell shoved Ryan against the wall, grabbed the back of his boxer shorts and tugged them up over Ryan's head. Ryan let out a shout as the fabric burned his backside.

'Leave you alone?' hissed Sarrell. 'Dream on, Jacobs. Never gonna happen. Someone's got to toughen you up.'

Sarrell let go and Ryan dropped to the floor. Before he could catch his breath, a hard kick left Ryan doubled over in pain.

With that, James Sarrell—now officially Devonmoor's bravest cadet—strode off, whistling.

***

When Mr Davids ambled into his office holding a mug of coffee, he was shocked to find Ryan sitting in his comfortable leather chair with his feet propped up on the desk.

Despite his fondness for the cadet, the teacher seemed annoyed at the invasion of his privacy. 'Ryan, my boy, what on earth are you doing? You can't make yourself at home in my office while I'm not here.'

Ryan smiled, put his hands behind his head, leaned back further and looked at the whiteboard. Mr Davids followed the boy's gaze to see that the numbers from the other day had been wiped off and replaced with neat lines of code.

'Well I guess if you've been working on the...' Mr Davids' voice trailed off. He took a step closer to the board, putting a hand out to steady himself on the desk. 'Is this...?' he asked, unable to finish the sentence.

Ryan nodded smugly.

The teacher sat down. 'But how did you...? Where did this come from?'

'Well, sir, you know how you say that I'm a computing genius?' said Ryan. 'It turns out, I am.'

Mr Davids read through the code again. He looked as though he was going to cry with happiness.

Ryan stood up. 'I think I'll leave you alone with it, sir.' he said. 'Enjoy.'

***

Dr Torren was not so easy to please.

After being summoned to his office, Ryan squirmed under the doctor's gaze.

'I know you were lying in Lady Devonmoor's office, Ryan. What I can't work out is why. Why let Sarrell take the credit?'

Ryan looked away. 'Me and Sarrell had a deal,' he admitted. 'It was the only way I could get him to work with me. I had to compromise. And that meant that he got to look good. He cares more about that stuff than I do.'

'But you approached Sarrell? You asked for his help?' Dr Torren leaned back in his chair, amused.

'Yep. That's what happened. But this is confidential, right? I don't want to break the deal we made. Not even now.'

'That's very honourable of you Jacobs,' nodded Dr Torren. 'Unless, of course, Sarrell is blackmailing you?'

Ryan felt himself going red. He didn't want anyone seeing the video footage of him suffering with the Fury. He'd never live it down. 'Maybe a little. What can I do?' Ryan looked up at the teacher, his eyes pleading. 'Don't make anything of this. Please, sir. I can handle it.'

'I see no reason anyone needs to know.'

Ryan relaxed in the comfortable leather chair.

'Besides,' added the doctor, 'I'm impressed you

realised you needed someone else's help instead of trying to deal with everything on your own. And especially that you chose to involve a person you don't like. That can't have been a straightforward decision.'

'It wasn't,' admitted Ryan. 'But after he pulled me through the tunnel on the assault course, I realised something. Sometimes you need someone like that: someone who's tough and cold and who doesn't care about people's feelings.'

'So, would you consider working with Cadet Sarrell again?'

'Honestly, sir?' said Ryan. 'I think I'd rather die. He hates me and I don't even know why.'

Dr Torren looked away. 'Sarrell has his own pain, Jacobs.'

'But he enjoys pain!' exclaimed Ryan. 'He basically asked the colonel to be extra harsh on him. I mean, why would anyone do that?'

'I can see why that would be a mystery to you.' The doctor smiled. 'But that doesn't mean he *enjoys* pain. Sarrell knows that pain makes us tougher. That's why he embraces it. He can't stand weakness.'

'But why?'

'Weakness killed his parents.'

They sat quietly for a moment as Ryan thought about that. 'Are you saying his parents were weak?'

'No. They were as tough as you get: undercover operatives, fiercely intelligent and highly skilled. They taught Sarrell to be like that, too. They worked as spies for our government until their cover was blown.'

'So how did weakness kill them?' Ryan was confused.

'Someone else's weakness. The person who betrayed them. Either for money, or because they were threatened. It's not clear which.'

'So, Sarrell hates weakness. I get it. But why take his pain out on me?'

'The traitor was a hacker, Jacobs.'

Now it made sense.

Ryan looked up at the doctor. 'He's never going to leave me alone, is he?'

'No,' admitted the doctor. 'Not unless you prove yourself and earn his trust.'

Ryan let out a long sigh. 'I think we both know that's never gonna happen.'

EPILOGUE

Rain poured down as Ryan splashed through the mud, hurtling towards the goal. He could score—just one swift kick and his team would be in the lead.

But Drew was on his left.

He glanced to the side, feeling a sudden rush of guilt as he caught sight of the ugly burn on Drew's cheek. The flare had scarred him for life.

'Jacobs, over here!'

Ryan cursed. But what could he do?

He passed the ball.

Drew took it forward, the opposing goalkeeper moving towards him to block the shot. But Drew didn't shoot. He slid the ball deftly back to Ryan. 'Shoot, Jacobs,' he yelled, 'and don't screw it up!'

Ryan didn't need telling twice. He sliced the ball into the back of the net, to the sound of cheers from his team. Drew ran over and gave him a high five.

'Thanks,' acknowledged Ryan. 'That was a great cross.'

Drew nodded.

'And,' added Ryan. 'I'm sorry for what happened to your face. I mean... I didn't mean to scar you... It was just...' He trailed off.

'Well,' Drew replied, 'for what it's worth, I never meant to try to kill you either, so how about we call it quits?'

'Sounds good to me.' Ryan turned back to the game, relieved to know that Drew wasn't holding any grudges.

And then he spotted her: Sarah Devonmoor, standing with a few other prefects at the sidelines, all sheltered under black umbrellas. She caught Ryan's eye as he looked in her direction.

He nodded, hoping that she might smile at him, or at least nod back.

But no. Nothing.

She was expressionless; impossible to read. Even Dr Torren wouldn't have been able to tell what she was thinking.

Ryan stood there in the pouring rain, water dripping from his rugby shirt, confused.

There was a sharp push from behind that almost knocked him face-first into the mud, but he managed to steady himself.

'What the—' He turned to see Kev running past.

'That was excellent play, mate, but get your head in the game.'

'Sure.'

It was good advice.

Devonmoor were in the lead with ten minutes to go; they were probably going to win. It was an important game: they were in the quarter-finals of the Academy Cup.

But for Ryan this game felt more important than it

did for the others.

This game *was* more important.

For the first time, Ryan had made it.

He'd been chosen to play on the school team.

And it felt good.

GET YOUR FREE E-BOOK

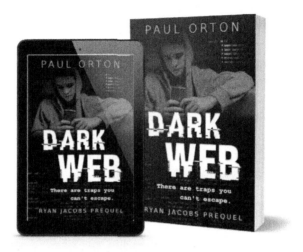

There are traps you can't escape.

When Ryan Jacobs asks to join the Faction he finds himself trapped in a situation which keeps getting worse. He needs to escape fast, or they will own him forever. But how can he fight an invisible enemy?

Find out about Ryan's life before he is taken to the Academy. DARK WEB is exclusively available to members of the Ryan Jacobs Alliance – sign up for free at www.paulorton.net

A NOTE FROM THE AUTHOR

Thanks for reading 'Wild Fury'. If you're up for more of Ryan's adventures, then check out the next book in the series: 'Code Zero'. In it, Ryan has some really difficult decisions to make that could cost him his place at the academy.

Maybe you'd also be interested in getting your hands on advanced copies of new books, before they even go on sale? If so then the readers' club is the place to start! Visit www.paulorton.net to join.

And could you do me a huge favour? I need you to review 'Wild Fury'. Reviews make a huge difference to a new author like me, and it would be amazing if you could write a sentence or two about what you liked about it. I'd really appreciate it and I promise I read every review.

Until next time,

Paul.

RYAN JACOBS BOOK 1

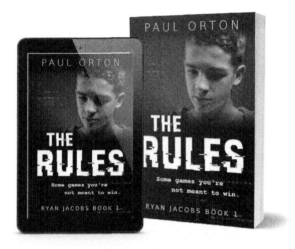

Somehow, he lost his freedom.

Now he belongs to the Academy, and the rules have changed. What started out as a game has become a matter of life and death.

If he doesn't think fast, someone will die.

At thirteen you shouldn't have to face these kinds of issues. But at thirteen, you don't get to decide the rules.

THE RULES is the first book in the Ryan Jacobs series and is <u>AVAILABLE NOW ON AMAZON</u>!

RYAN JACOBS BOOK 3

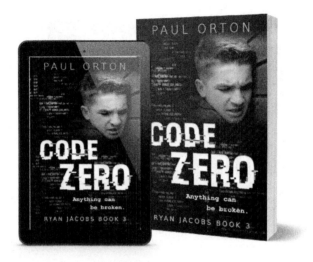

There's something in the woods.
And it's out of control.

When Ryan realises the danger, he has a difficult
decision to make: it's not easy to own up to your
mistakes when you're already in so much trouble.
But if he doesn't sort it out fast, someone could die.
Will he be able to tame the technology before
anyone is killed? Or will he confess and lose his
place at the academy? At thirteen, it's a harsh
choice. But, this time, he only has himself to blame.

**CODE ZERO is the third book in the Ryan Jacobs
series and is <u>AVAILABLE NOW ON AMAZON</u>!**

RYAN JACOBS BOOK 4

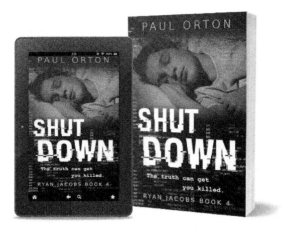

Everyone has secrets.
Even those you least expect.

Ryan is in trouble. He has to stop the shutdown but doesn't know who to trust. The authorities are closing in and he's running out of time. It's not easy being thirteen and having a reputation. Whatever he does, his enemies are one step ahead. But if he doesn't succeed, more innocent people will die. Will he uncover the truth? And will anyone believe him when he does, or will it just get him killed?

SHUT DOWN is the fourth book in the Ryan Jacobs series and is <u>AVAILABLE NOW ON AMAZON!</u>

Printed in Great Britain
by Amazon

22705512R00101